T0078287

ANNIHILATION:
ALMOST

ANNIHILATION:
ALMOST
TIME TO START AGAIN

RAJ

PARTRIDGE
A Penguin Random House Company

Copyright © 2013 by Raj.

ISBN: Hardcover   978-1-4828-1485-9
              Softcover   978-1-4828-1483-5
              Ebook   978-1-4828-1484-2

To order additional copies of this book, contact
Partridge India
000 800 10062 62
www.partridgepublishing.com/india
orders.india@partridgepublishing.com

CONTENTS

Dear Pari,

I would like to dedicate this book to you as it would have been impossible for me to work on it without your support, patience and understanding. You are my pillar of strength and I would forever be indebted to you for standing with me in difficult times.

With love and respect,

Raj

"I was not made by the God

He (just) sent me
to be called his son,"
he said to me.

"It did not make me either

He (just) sent me
to be called a Man,"
I replied.

Hi.

I am Robin. It is not my real name though. It is my pseudo that I adopted during my days as an "e-Vigilante"; a name that I adopted when I started fighting crime online in the final year of high school. I took this name from the fictional character 'Robin hood'. And, that was before I joined the CIA.

Today, I am at a position where I am responsible for everything that happens in this world and people look up to me for the growth and progress of the society. But, that is today. I led quite a different life a few years ago. This book is about how my life changed a few years ago and took me on the path that led me to my current status today.

I will start off from December 2015 when I was still in college completing my 'MS' from one of the top institutes in the world, which was located in north-eastern United States, and, would take you through my journey with the CIA that started with one of the, sorry, not one of the but THE biggest computer-project ever undertaken by mankind, and, ended in a way that I couldn't have imagined, in fact no one could have imagined, even in my wildest dreams. But, it did happen and it changed the course of not only my life, but, it changed the course of LIFE.

I am writing about my journey to tell the future generations how we ended up where we are today, what were the mistakes we committed and what lessons did we learn from that journey; and, how we incorporated those lessons into our world to shape our world the way it is today.

THE BEGINNING
OF A NEW LIFE

THE ENTRY

Up until about the first twenty-five years of my life, my biggest accomplishment was getting selected to the annals of one of the most prestigious institutes in the world in the field of Computer Studies, which had continuously been accorded a place in the top three in that field over the years.

But, something happened in my last semester that changed everything for me and about me.

*   *   *

I was supposed to be a Computer Network and Security Specialist. But, I used to dabble in almost everything related to computers. However, what was different about me was that I was an "e-Vigilante". That was a new term that I came up with. As a young child, I used to read a lot of comics and used to think, like any other child with fantasies, that I would be a vigilante, a crime fighter, some day and would save common people from criminals. However, as I grew up, I realized how childish my thoughts were and how far from reality. But, all the years that I spent working in the digital world brought me face to face with the reality that there were a lot of bad guys out there in the digital world trying to make use of their computer skills to make some quick bucks at the expense of the lives of others, including their money and their security. I believed, and I still believe, that everyone who uses his technical skills to cause disruption or destruction should be paid back in the same currency. 'Hacking' is just like a gun. In wrong hands, it can only effect a crime, but, in the right hands, it can act as a means of defense, of security and of protection.

And, keeping that in mind, I decided to be in the digital world what I could not be in the real world. I used to spend any free time I had on my hand trying to watch the internet, keeping a look out for any attempted hacking and to prevent it and report it. I started doing it in the final year of high school. However, by the second year of graduation, I started realizing that I wasn't making any considerable contribution by the methods I was using. Yes, I was a good hacker, and my methods were top-shelf, but, still, I couldn't monitor the whole internet twenty-four hours a day and definitely not the private networks. I also realized that the most danger to the society was by the hackers who used to break into government networks to either disrupt them or to steal important data from them, or from those who would steal financial data from banks and card companies.

To have a more effective approach and system to counter such hackers, I worked hard and developed a method that proved to be extremely effective and fruitful for me. The new method developed by me allowed me to keep an eye on all major networks without actually sitting on my computer and monitoring everything on my own. And, not only that, it took over the system's defenses and became the first line of defense against a hack attack on a system by creating a screen between the system's defenses and the attacking files. It did not stop the system's defenses from fighting the intruder, but, it created a second front with an alternative approach and, thus, bolstered the defense mechanism of that system.

My new method was based on the concept of leaving digital **"BUOYS"** on major networks and channels at various strategic points. By strategic locations I mean certain access channels that any intruder would need to pass through in order to take control or simply to enter. Think of it as a multistory building with a gate at every level and with several apartments at each level with each apartment having several doors for each room. Thus, to reach a particular room in that building, a person would need to pass through several doors to reach the floor where the room is, and, then, through the door of that particular apartment, and, finally, through the door of that room. In the same way, any intruder into a network has to pass through certain access points, and, those were the locations that I picked to plant my **"BUOYS"**. Those **"BUOYS"** were designed to send out an alert to me about any attempt at an intrusion into that network or any part of that network. Simultaneously, they used to alert the network administrators about the intrusion. I called them **"BUOYS"** not only because they used to alert me in case of intrusions like the ones used at sea as markers, but, also because I had built a floating mechanism in them like the ones used at sea. They would hide themselves in a file and in case a system's defense mechanism initiated any scan to locate the infected file, the **"BUOY"** would detach itself from that file and would keep hopping from file to file and if the number of scanned files got much larger than the ones still pending to be scanned, it would jump to one of the files already scanned. Those **"BUOYS"** were complex codes that I had designed on my own with main focus on ability and stealth. Whenever, I would target a system with them, they would enter the system cloaked as an update to the security system, but, with a jumbled code hidden inside the file. Being jumbled, the system never took it as a program that could threaten its security. However, once the mail file had found a place to fix itself, it would un-jumble the sentences in the hidden code to form the intended code and would release that into the system.

Most of the networks and sites at that time had enough protection to fend off small attacks and attempts at Password cracking with Brute Force techniques or Hashing algorithms. However, when it came to high-end hackers who were much more adept at breaking into a system or a network, using a bundle of ever-evolving techniques, almost all networks were fallible. The methods to fight hacking had evolved over the years but had not been able to keep up with those of the opponents.

My **"BUOYS"** were not mere signaling devices. They also acted as the first line of defense against any threat. Whenever someone introduced a Virus or a Worm into a network to disrupt the network or to penetrate it or to create a backdoor, the **"BUOYS"** acted in the manner similar to an antibody reaction in a human body in response to a viral or a bacterial infection. The **"BUOYS"** generated certain sequences that attached themselves to the incoming program and either rendered it meaningless or created unending loops. At the same time, they used to pull out all the information about that program's source and its path as can possibly be retrieved, and would send it to me and the network's administrators. The defense mechanism was quite similar to any adopted by an anti-virus program or a firewall. The only difference was that it was much more powerful and much more effective compared to them. I planted them in various networks and no one could detect their presence or realize what they were doing. There was another function served by them but I never utilized them for that. Though their primary function was defense, I had created them in such a way that they could be used for offense as well. Had I ever intended to take over a network, I simply had to introduce a switch mechanism and the **"BUOYS"** would have triggered a take-over from inside while I would have attacked from the outside, and would have neutralized all the defense mechanisms and, all of it would have happened without tripping any alarms. Thus, I could have gained control and administration of a network in a "Ghost Mode".

Anyways, forgetting about the computer mumbo jumbo, let me take you forward to what happened. I kept refining my technique and kept beating one hacker after another and gave a lot of information to the concerned authorities anonymously resulting in a number of arrests in a number of countries. I continued doing that for more than two years and during that period, my pseudo name 'ROBIN' became extremely famous in the digital world. A lot of articles were written about me and my achievements on the net. I was a sort of cyber celebrity. However, no one ever came to know about Robin's (mine) real identity up until a stupid mistake on my part. After successfully thwarting an attack on a major government-operated network, I boasted about it to one of my nerd friends. I could not keep it to me. I was elated and could not resist the temptation to share it with someone. At that time, I did not think it would be a big deal. But, as luck would have it, it turned out to be a BIG deal. My friend got inspired and decided to go my way. There is no doubt in my mind that he was, maybe still is, good at programming but he was definitely not in the big league (and I'm not trying to boast here). His **"BUOYS"** were not perfect and did not pass through the systems undetected. The network that was his first target had top of the line defense and it perceived it as an attempt at intrusion. After all, unlike me, he had not tested his **"BUOYS"** with an easy target and went straight to hit a network owned by a Federal Intelligence agency. And, as expected, the Feds showed up at his door and took him in. When they questioned him, he quickly gave them my name as the real master whom he had tried to copy. The Feds picked me up as well. But, I explained myself to them and gave them information about how I had helped out the government discreetly by thwarting off attacks on its networks and by giving anonymous tips about the hackers involved in such cyber attacks. It is good that I have a strong memory which enabled me to give precise details to them. Upon checking out the information given by me, they brought me out of the interrogation room and took me to a conference room where I waited for a few minutes before my interrogating officer entered accompanied by another man who clearly was his superior. I was confused about why was I in the conference room. The senior officer told me that after investigating into my claims, they had found out that all the details give by me were absolutely correct, and, that they had decided to offer me a position in the FBI as a Cyber-Expert. I could not think of a reason not to accept that offer and gladly agreed to work with them.

However, since I had not completed my MS by then, I asked them to allow me time to complete my studies before joining the FBI in the role offered to me. They agreed to that easily as it was only a three-month period.

*   *   *

I went through that three month period with a mixture of emotions of unease at the long wait and excitement at the prospect of joining the Federal Bureau of Investigation (FBI) right after the finals and about becoming a "Fed" and wearing the jacket with FBI written on the back. But, I for sure did not know what was in store for me.

On the day my examination ended, towards the end of March 2016, I came out of the college building while discussing the paper with my friends and a couple of well-built guys in suits walked up to me and asked me to walk with them to their car (at which they pointed at a black car with tinted windows parked about a hundred yards away) to talk to their boss who was waiting in the car for me. I was a bit apprehensive as I did not know who they were. They could sense my hesitation and one of them smiled and told me it was about my job as a technical expert. At that, I assumed it was someone from the FBI who had come to meet me and hire me as my finals were over and done with. So, I went with the two of them over to the car. One of them opened the door at the rear left of the car and asked me to hop in. inside the car, there was a forty-something gentleman waiting for me who welcomed me with a warm smile. The two men who had escorted me came in and sat in the front and we drove off. I did not know for sure where was I being taken to but I assumed the destination to be the local FBI office. However, my assumption was incorrect.

The gentleman, who was sitting in the back with me, introduced himself as Daniel Steyn. At first, he made some small talk about how my exams went and how was life for the previous three months. He also asked me about my work against Cyber attacks and attackers. Here, I must tell you that I have an extremely expressive face, and, I can never hide my real emotions from other people. I say this because I am pretty sure that Mr. Steyn was able to read the questions in my mind on my face as he suddenly stopped talking for a few seconds.

"You must be wondering who I am and where am I taking you to," said Mr. Steyn, breaking the awkward silence, and continued, "I . . . . am not from the FBI. Let me introduce myself properly. I am Daniel Steyn, Assistant Director, Cyber Support, CIA. We heard about your little encounter with the Feds. At that time, we were already looking for the person who had secretly and anonymously helped us on more than a dozen occasions and had also helped us and the Feds nab more than a dozen cyber-attackers. We were looking for the Ghost, the Phantom, the mystery man, as my team called you."

At that point, I couldn't help but utter in shock, "CIA! You are from the CIA"

"Yes. I am from the CIA and I had been waiting for the last three months to meet you," replied Mr. Steyn. "We came to know about you from our sources in the FBI and when we matched in information given by you with that in our records, we realized that you were the prize we were after," he added further.

"But what do you want from me Mr. Steyn? As far as I know, you wouldn't go through the trouble of a three-month wait and coming over to see me just to put your stamp on me instead of the FBI. I am quite sure it is not a hiring competition that you are looking to win," said I.

A smile came and lingered on his face for a couple of seconds, and, then, he said, "I was kind of expecting this. A smart person like you would come up with smart questions and logical deductions. That is what is expected of you. And yes, I did not come here just to make you a part of the CIA to go one-up on some inter-agency rivalry. It is much bigger than that."

At that point, the car suddenly stopped. I looked out the window to see where we had reached, and found out that we were just outside the building where I had been staying on rent for the previous three years. My first and immediate reaction was to look back at Mr. Steyn with a questioning look.

To my unasked question, he replied, "Go and get your stuff. We are going on a small trip. Just bring a couple of pairs of clothes and other necessary items for now. We don't need to travel heavy. Jonathan here would help you (pointing at the guy in the front passenger seat)."

"Where are we going?" I could not help but asking.

"The Pentagon"

At the Pentagon

I had never, not even in my wildest dreams, imagined about working with the CIA and going to the Pentagon for work. But, there I was, entering the second-most important building in the United States after the White House, walking toe to toe with the Assistant Director, Cyber Support, CIA.

He took me to what appeared to be a medium-sized conference room. He asked me to wait there for a few minutes. I am quite sure that I did not have to wait for more than fifteen minutes, but, every minute seemed to last for at least an hour. The white walls in the 15'-10' room were as bare as they could be with only a map of Unites States on one of the walls and a projection screen on one wall. It wasn't usual for me to tense up in situations but 'that' was an exception. The temperature in the room was quite comfortable but, still, I could feel my armpits dampening with sweat. There was a dryness that was gradually taking over my throat and after clearing my throat thrice, I decided to get up and look for water. But, as soon as I got up, Mr. Steyn entered the room followed by two others. One of them looked to be in the same age bracket as Mr. Steyn but the other seemed at least a decade older. Mr. Reese handed me a bottle of water while he sat down on a chair near me while the other two sat across the table from us.

"Let me make the introductions," began Mr. Steyn and continued, "This is Mr. James McCracken, Director, Inter-agency Relations, and, (pointing to the comparatively younger man) this is Mr. Nathan Pattison, Director, Network Control. These are the two most important gentlemen in the division to which I belong." Then, addressing the two of them, he said, "And, here is ROBIN, the Ghost who has been helping us for the last two years without being a part of our organization. The Ghost, the Phantom, the Shadow whom our men could not locate, leave alone catch." The two of them sat there stone-faced. I had never seen anyone with as much lack of expression as those two. There wasn't any appreciation, any disdain, any acknowledgment, anything.

Then, Mr. Steyn turned his attention back to me. "I am sure you must be wondering about what is it that WE want from you as a member of our organization. Now, it is a fact that you have been working under the radar for the last two years, at least, escaping detection not only from our specialists but also the rogue hackers all over the world. Had it not been for your good friend, we might have never found out about you. What impressed us most was the fact that even though you were present everywhere, there was no digital signature that you had left anywhere, no bread crumbs, no footprints, nothing. And, that is what we are looking for in our cyber experts. Now, our experts are actual experts and amongst the best in the game. But, the problem is that like any other agency in the world, all of them are good at offense. They are hard-hitters going straight into open attacks and launch themselves massively. But, the problem with this approach is that every opponent that we face uses the same approach be it the R_____s, the C_____e, the P____s, or anyone else, and, as a result we accord them as much space to infiltrate as they give us. But, you . . . . You are different. You have a strong multi-pronged defense that ultimately ensnares the opponent and strangulates him without revealing your identity or anything about you. Our experts have studied your method and as per them, it is to cyber-defense what Stealth jets are to the Air Force."

He, then, took a slight pause, looked over at the other two seated across the table, and, continued, "We would like you to join our Cyber Task Force that has been created with an aim to strengthen our defense measures. After all, our networks are the most attacked networks in the world. It is an elite group that we are creating by hand-picking some of the best computer experts and, since you have proved yourself to be the best of the best, we would like you to be a part of it. The fact that you had agreed to be a part of the FBI told us that you intend to use your skills for the benefit of our country. Therefore, we are offering you this opportunity, which is even bigger for you as far as using your skills is concerned and the amount of resources available to you. You would have unlimited resources at your disposal, latest technology, fastest computers, and a combined intellect of some of the best minds in the country. Now it is up to you to decide whether you would like to go to the big league or start off with the minors."

My heart was beating much faster than usual and was pushing me to go ahead and jump up and grab the opportunity, but, my mind was still thinking over it. There was a long silence in the room with three pairs of eyes looking at me earnestly.

"Take your time. We will just come back in a few minutes," said Mr. Steyn and got up to go out of the room along with the others. But, even before he could completely get up from his seat, I blurted out quite suddenly, "I will do it. Count me in."

A big smile stretched itself on Mr. Steyn's face as he looked at the other two who nodded in affirmative perhaps giving a go ahead to Mr. Steyn for his plans. He got up and stretched out his hand to shake mine.

"But, I have a condition," I said without shaking his outstretched hand.

"And, what would that be?" asked Daniel while taking his hand back.

"I have never worked on anyone else's terms. I work on my own terms. I would like to be the boss of my work," I replied.

"We wanted to keep it that way in any case. You would head the programming team of our new project. You would not be answering to anyone except me, and I, in turn, would be answerable to my bosses. So, if you are okay with this arrangement, I would like to welcome you aboard," he said, and, stretched out his hand to shake mine.

And, that time, I accepted that outstretched hand to express my consent.

And that was the beginning of my life with the intelligence services. In fact, it was the beginning of an adventure that I am still living.

*   *   *

Since it was the first time I had been to the Pentagon, I obviously did not know much about the building and what all was done there. What I definitely did not know, and I am sure not many people knew, about was the existence of an underground network deep below the Pentagon. However, it took me about a year's hard work to prove myself worthy enough to be introduced to that WORLD. On my first day, I followed Mr. Steyn like a lost puppy looking all around with wide eyes, amazed at the size of the structure and the huge number of people I could see all around.

The Pentagon was a huge five storey structure made up of five concentric pentagonal rings (designated A, B, C, D and E rings) that enclosed a big five-acre open courtyard. There were ten spike-like corridors that divided the whole structure into ten divisions. There were two below-ground levels as well namely the BASEMENT and the MEZZANINE. Mr. Steyn told me that more than 25,000 people worked in that building in various departments and divisions of the government. It had five facades: the Mall Terrace Entrance facade, the River Terrace Entrance facade, the Concourse Entrance (or Metro Station) facade, the South Parking Entrance facade, and the Heliport facade. And, quite obviously since it housed some of the most important divisions of the Department of Defense and other agencies, most of the offices lacked windows. Mr. Steyn was quite a friendly person and talkative as well. He told me a lot about the building while he went through his usual business and while we were waiting for approvals for me. He told me about the "Purple Water Fountain" in the 08th Corridor on the Mezzanine level; about the "Bomber Bar" (a bar exclusively for the Air Force Pilots and honored guests); and a lot many things I never knew about. At around 1600 hours, the building appeared quite deserted compared to the day, as the masses rolled out by that time.

While I was following Mr. Steyn all around, I started observing him much more closely. Till that time, I had been lost in my thoughts and the confusions to actually pay much attention to him and his personality. However, my first day of orientation gave me enough time to observe him. He was not a big man, 5'10" at the maximum, but was well built. I did not know his age at that time but could easily assume that he was no less than forty-five years of age. Clean-shaven but with a lot of Grey sprinkled all over his head in such a manner that it told the other people that the silver was not due to age but most probably by experience. He carried himself well but I could not help but notice the slightly drooping shoulders and his tendency to continuously lose himself in his thoughts and come back to the world with a jerk. A good smattering of crisscross lines all over his face often forced others to miscalculate his age and take him to be much older than his real age. He was wearing a good suit, which was not top of the line but was decent enough. I always thought, and I still believe it to be true, that he wore a pair of spectacles not because he needed it but to hide his eyes from a clear observation because his eyes were a clear giveaway to his thoughts and feelings. His face was usually within his control, but his eyes, they were a different story altogether.

All during the day, there was one question that kept cropping up and hovering around in my mind, which was, "Why were we at the Pentagon and not at the CIA headquarters?" After all, we were to work on some project for the CIA. We left the Pentagon around 1700 hours, and by that time my curiosity had taken the best of me and I could not control myself anymore. While sitting at a table in a restaurant which Mr. Steyn said was amongst the best low-budget eatery in DC, I popped up the question finally:

"I thought we would be going to Langley but instead of doing that we ended up spending time at the Pentagon and that too without doing anything. Is there anything I am missing in all this Mr. Steyn?"

"I have been waiting for this question since the morning. I am quite surprised that you did not ask this the whole day. If it is because you feel hesitant talking to me or asking about stuff from me, let me assure you that I am your boss only for operational purposes and you can consider me as your friend off the paper. Let's start off with taking away the formalities between us. From now on, do not address me formally. You can call me Daniel. As for your question, there are a lot of things that I have to tell you and a lot of information that you need to process in your brain. I took you to the Pentagon because that is where our new offices would be and I wanted you to get comfortable with the surroundings and not get overawed by the building or the people working there."

"So what exactly would we be working on?" I couldn't help but asking.

"We would be working on a lot of things. For starters, let me tell you a bit more about our new division. I am sure you are aware of the various agencies in the intelligence sphere like the CIA, the FBI, the DIA, the NSA, the NRO, Homeland Security, amongst others. Now all these agencies, including ours, have their own networks and communications systems that are managed by their respective experts. However, a huge increase in attacks from hackers has proved our facilities to be inadequate. Speaking in plain words, none of them are strong enough. The opponents are gaining strength by the day and we are falling behind by huge margins. So, the top heads have decided to bring everything under one roof. Once our whole group comes together, we would be managing all the networks and all the data present in each and every computer owned by the US government on this planet. We would be the ones protecting all that data. You can easily imagine the importance of all that data. We would be protecting details of top-secret projects, military installations, army bases, science projects undertaken by the Army, etc. etc. In short, we would be the new guardians of the country."

"So, would we be the part of CIA or this new organization?"

"In its more than a hundred year old history, the CIA has been formed of four directorates, the Directorate of Intelligence, the National Clandestine Service, the Directorate of Support, and, the Directorate of Science and Technology. Similarly, there are separate divisions within NSA as well. Now, there would be a new division that would be carved out of the Directorate of Support and the Directorate of Science and Technology from CIA and similar wings from the NSA, which would be called the Directorate of Network Administration or DNA for short. We would be a part of that division. However, the headquarters of that division would neither be at Langley (CIA headquarters) or Fort Meade (NSA headquarters). We would be operating out of CYBERIA . . ."

"CYBERIA?"

"Yes, Cyberia. It is spelt C-Y-B-E-R-I-A. It is the name of the project site where we would work alongside resources from other intelligence agencies, from the Armed Forces and the Research wings. That project site is located at level B-6 (B Minus Six or Six levels below the Basement) of the Pentagon . . . ."

"B-6? I thought the lowest level was the Basement," I said almost incredulously.

"Well, for the world, Basement is the lowest level of the pentagon. However, there are six other levels located below the basement. After the infamous "9/11" attacks on the Pentagon fifteen years ago, there were some structural changes that were made in the building. It was strengthened, fortified, and various other security measures were put in place. There were six additional levels built below the basement that not only house some super sensitive research and intelligence projects, but, can also act as bunkers in case of a future attack. In that attack, a large number of people had died as there were no proper bunkers to escape the destruction and whatever little places that the people hid themselves in after the attacks were absolutely inaccessible after the attacks as all access points got blocked by debris and due to some other problems like the low height of the access tunnels preventing the entry of fire trucks till their tops were cut off. By the time the rescue personnel got to those people, half of them had died due to lack of air supply, or bleeding or smoke, etc. Therefore, when these new levels were built, a fail-safe was built there. Certain sensors were installed throughout the structure that are programmed to get activated in case of an attack on the Pentagon, and, subsequently, about half-an-hour after the attack, to initiate the collapse of a particular stretch of land creating an exit path opening out about two miles away from the Pentagon. Once opened, the passageway can be closed using a heavily encrypted digital passkey and a password that are in the possession of the Secretary of State and the Chief of Staff, respectively. And, one of them has to be at Langley and the other person has to be at the Pentagon for the purpose."

I could never have known about these things about the Pentagon had I not decided to be a part of that new project.

After that, we spent a week at the Pentagon, which I thoroughly utilized in gathering knowledge about the Who's Who and the functioning of various organizations.

In Daniel's words, "The project would take at least a year to be operational and by that time, you would need to know about each and every person involved in the project and everything about their lives. You also need to know everything about everyone who matters at the Pentagon, Langley and most importantly, the White House."

And, I did just that. That one year was definitely well-spent as far as gathering knowledge about others was concerned.

*   *   *

After spending a year at Langley, Daniel took me to our project site CYBERIA, located at level "B-6" at the Pentagon, in April 2017. We first went to the Basement level which was known to everyone. However, what no one knew about was the presence of a secret passageway at the Western edge. The entrance was not easily visible and the entry-point leading to the gallery, at the end of which the entrance lay, was guarded round the clock, with no entry to any unauthorized personnel.

The entrance had a double-door access. At the first door, certain hidden sensors used to automatically conduct a facial scan and a body-scan and used to match the two with the photographic records maintained on a server that was managed from inside CYBERIA. While the system matched the records, it also opened up the complete profile, of the person trying to obtain access, for use at the second door. Once across the first door, one used to come to the second door that had a central panel that opened up only when the first door had closed down completely. That panel conducted a Five-point scan on the person.

First was the Fingerprint Scan; Second, the Iris Scan; Third, Tongue impression scan; Fourth, Heart-beat Scan; and, lastly, the DNA Scan. All those scans were based on the fact that those five factors are unique to each and every individual. The first scan was quite easy and routine wherein the person sanitized his hands using a solution kept at a corner specifically for the purpose, and, held up his hand with palm facing the scanner and the scanner scanned and matched the prints with the ones stored in the profile of the person. In the second scan, one used to place his face on a holder to get his eyes in line with the scanner that scanned the Irises of the person. Simultaneously, one had to give the tongue impression on a scanner located just below the Iris Scanner and the face hold. Another scanner fixed itself to the left chest of the person to scan the heart-beat pattern of the person. At the same time, the person had to put a finger of his left hand, or any other part of the hand, over a scan machine with a prick-needle. The needle used to pinch the finger to obtain a blood sample and immediately transferred the sample obtained to a DNA profiler that obtained and analyzed the DNA sample with the ones stored in the person's profile. The scans took effect only if all of them were done simultaneously. The whole process took about ten minutes during which the person could relax on the lounger kept there.

Upon crossing the second door, a passageway used to open up that had three lifts on each side. Each lift led to a specific level only and had no access to any other level, i.e. there was a lift each for B-1, B-2, B-3, B-4, B-5 and B-6. There were no markings on any of the lifts. Without any markings, it was not possible for anyone to know which lift led to which level unless someone from the organization provided that information. Then, each lift could be opened only with the help of access codes that were specific to each and every individual working on that particular level, and those codes were changed every day on a random basis. Every day when a person left the facility, he or she obtained the password for the next day from the server and had to use that to leave the premises and enter the next day.

On my first visit to CYBERIA project site, I was simply overwhelmed by the sheer size of the site. The elevator opened into a multitude of cabins that had no name tabs at that time as they had not been allocated to anyone till then. After walking about three hundred (300) meters through a maze flanked by cabins on both sides, we reached a huge open space, which was central to the whole site plan and at least a hundred (100) meters away from any edge of the site with plenty of cabins, labs and other rooms built in between. As per what Daniel had told me at that time and from what I gathered during my time spent associated with the project, I can tell you that the total size of the facility was approximately One Hundred and Fifty Thousand (1,50,000) Square Meters and was divided into various sections. The point where the elevator opened up was the Administrative section housing all administrative and support personnel like the Procurement Specialists; towards the right end of the site was the Security section where two security experts were available round the clock to monitor each and every person entering and exiting the premises as well as those working within the premises though most of their work was later handled by our Supercomputer and they were simply to watch; towards the extreme back, in the left hand corner, there was a Cooling plant that maintained an optimal temperature for the

Supercomputer as well as the rest of the site; towards the right hand corner of the extreme back (exactly opposite to the cooling plant) were the back-up generators and fuel cells that automatically kicked-in in case the power from the main supply station stopped (which never happened except once); in between those two was a tunnel that led to the main Power Supply Station located about Two kilometers away in another underground location built specifically to support B-1 to B-6; in that tunnel, at almost the mid-way point, there was the Water Storage and Pumping facility for B-1 to B-6; and exactly at the center of the site was the space which was the focus of the project.

"This is where 'CYBERION-I' would be located," said Daniel, pointing at the empty space at the center of the site.

CYBERION-1

"Tomorrow you would meet the rest of the team that would be working on the project," said Daniel and continued, "In fact everyone would be meeting everyone else for the first time. At the moment, there are only four people who know about the complete team; I, two of my Superiors, and, their boss. The total team comprises of seventy-six people with a multitude of specialties. There are Cyber-Experts like yourself; Hardware Specialists; Procurement Specialists who can arrange for anything that might be required for the project no matter how difficult it might be to get that thing, right from a pin to a plane, from a bullet to a missile and from a pen to a satellite; experts on Chemistry, Biology and other sciences; experts who can handle any kind of machinery; and Language Experts among others."

And as Daniel had said, the complete team was brought to the site one by one with the last of the members pouring in almost seven hours after the first one. In addition to the seventy-six of us, there were fifty-six support and maintenance staff members as well who were a part of the project.

Once everyone had arrived, Daniel went up on a podium and started introducing everyone, one by one, to the rest of the team. I must say that I was mighty impressed by the fact that Daniel did not need any files or papers or anything else to introduce anyone. He simply knew everything about everyone. Seventy-six members of the core team and fifty-six members of the support staff. One hundred and thirty-two (132) names. One hundred and thirty-two faces. One hundred and thirty-two profiles with personal details, educational backgrounds and professional histories. And, he did not falter even once. Moreover, it did not seem that he had memorized anything as he kept moving from one person to another as smoothly as possible. You can imagine my feelings at this by the fact that once the introductions were over, I couldn't recollect even half of the names let alone putting the names and the faces together.

Once Daniel had completed all the introductions of the Core team and the support staff, he moved on to introduce his superiors to whom he reported directly, Mr. Jonathan Flinchard and Mr. Paul Weinardt. Mr. Flinchard was Joint Director (Intelligence), NSA, and, Mr. Weinardt was Joint Director (Cyber Support), CIA. Finally, Daniel introduced their boss, Mr. James D Rourke, Chief Security Advisor to the President.

Then, it was Mr. Rourke's turn to address the team.

"I would like to thank you all for agreeing to be the part of this project, CYBERION-1. I am sure all of you were told that this is the biggest Cyber-Security project ever undertaken by any government in the world. However, that's not the whole story. In fact, it is not even a part of the whole story. It is merely the beginning of the story.

When Daniel (pointing at Daniel) contacted you to be a part of this project, you were just a prospect and, hence, we couldn't reveal too much to you. But now, you are a part of the project, a part of the organization, a part of us. Therefore, I believe it is time to tell all of you a bit more about the project. This project site, CYBERIA, would house the fastest Supercomputer on the planet with the largest digital storage space. This supercomputer, "CYBERION-I", would be the hub of all government-owned computer networks in the United States and its offshore territories and bases, both at state-level and federal. Nothing new or big. Isn't it? But wait, that's not all. It would also establish a phantom link to all kinds of private networks existing in the country. Then, we would move to other private networks around the globe and, finally, all government owned networks of each and every nation. In short, we would hack into everything computer in this world and leave our presence there to keep a track of everything happening all over the world. We would be present in each and every computer, and through that, each and every computer, every satellite, every plane, every train, every ship, every security camera, every digital camera, etc. No one would know we are watching them or keeping an eye on them. We would monitor everything happening everywhere. And, before anyone of you may ask the reason for all this, let me give you the answer."

After a brief pause and a sip of water from a glass, he continued, "we are living in a world that is moving away from the age-old concepts of launching an invasion or attack using men and weapons resulting in huge costs both in terms of men and money. We moved from stones to swords, from swords to guns, from guns to tanks, from tanks to planes, from bullets to missiles, and from dynamite to nuclear bombs. But now, in a world that is more or less dependent on computers to function properly and effectively, everything is moving from the real world to the digital world, including WAR. This is the age of the beginning of Cyber-warfare, and, we want to be the ones to be the first to assume total supremacy in this war. There are rogue nations out there who wish to use the cyberspace to cause havoc financially, operationally, and in every other possible way. We have decided that we cannot let this happen. We need to control it and gradually put a stop to all of it. Therefore, we thought of "CYBERION-I". Using this, we would keep an eye on the digital as well as the real world and would intercept any plan of any form of attack whether a terrorist attack in the real world, wherever it might be, or a cyber-attack wherever it might be. Till date, we have helped various nations by providing them support against tyranny, terrorism, and war using the tools of diplomacy, force and money. Now, once this project is fully functional, we would be the vigilantes saving the world from destruction."

He culminated his speech at such a crescendo that a nice round of applause was quite obvious. I wasn't really sure if he had told us everything there was to know about the project or whether such honest intentions were actually the intentions that the government intended to put into effect once the project was functional. But, the way he said it, even I, the perennial skeptic, was forced to applaud.

We spent the next one year working at completing the installation of "CYBERION-I", the behemoth of the computer world. During that one year, we realized that it was not merely a computer; it was an attempt at Artificial Intelligence at a much grander scale than ever attempted.

Even though the core team and the support team comprised of people with diverse backgrounds, ethnicity, qualifications, talents, capabilities, and, experiences, all of us blended together to such an extent that the project ran ahead of schedule and all the systems were put in place with almost a month in hand.

Let me tell you a bit about our supercomputer "CYBERION-1".

The total size of the Core System Unit was twenty-five thousand Square Meters. The system consisted of **1,60,000** Computer Nodes comprising of a total of **3,12,00,000** Cores. And, it was not simply a giant bulk of machinery. It was the fastest computer system ever built at that time, and, no one has attempted such a machine after it (I will come to the reason of that later). The fastest supercomputer prior to our behemoth had a peak operating speed of **107 PetaFLOPS**. At that time, there were attempts going on the world over to create a machine that could scale the **500 PetaFLOPS** level. However, we had the best of technology at our hands. There were certain Chips that were specifically designed by the scientists and researchers at the DoD (Department of Defense) and were produced by one of the leading Chip Manufacturers on a secret basis only for our project. No one before or after us had access to that kind of technology. I would not bore you with exact and minute details of the chip and its layout, but, I can tell you that it was a definite and major improvement over the **"Ivy-Bridge"** layout in use at that time in most supercomputers in operation at the time. The only factor that was in consonance with the other supercomputers of the time was the 'Interconnect' that utilized a **'Fat Tree Topology'**. Using the technological advancements put into operation only for our project, we created the system with a speed of **1.5 ExaFLOPS** (1 ExaFLOPS = 10^{18} FLOPS (Floating Point Operations Per Second)). The total memory of the system, including the CPU and GPU memory, stood at **2048 PiB** (Pebibyte). Despite the huge size and the lighting speed, the system was built in quite an energy efficient manner and was definitely not a power guzzler like many of its predecessors. Its energy efficiency was calculated at **7800 LINPACK MFLOPS / WATT**. The total power consumption of the complete project site, including the Computer System Unit, stood at a whopping **200 MW**.

The operational control room comprised of a huge room with one wall completely built of glass to overlook the system as it gave a complete view of the system from overhead. The wall directly opposite to the glass wall was decked with computer screens with nothing of the wall visible. In the huge panel of screens, there were three big screens silhouetted by sixteen smaller ones. Those three were named, quite unimaginatively, **Primary Monitor 1 (PM1), Primary Monitor 2 (PM2) and Primary Monitor 3 (PM3)**. All major messages from the system used to flash on **PM2**. **PM1** and **PM3** were for deeper analysis for every red flag put up by the system against major criminal activities.

We had already run initial and mandatory tests on the system and it had come out with flying colors. However, the extra time allowed us to conduct much more thorough and varied tests to check for any glitches and to test the true potential of the system.

Daniel arranged for some serious attacks, on a certain government-owned defense network, by some rogue hackers who were amongst the best on the dark side of the fence. They were paid a good amount to get them to arrange for their team and launch a full-bloodied massive attack. I am sure that even Howard and his superiors might not have expected as strong an offensive as launched by them. However, "CYBERION-I" proved to be too smart for them. We had no idea where were they going to strike and Daniel gave us no indications or hints to that effect whatsoever. But, it did not matter. The moment the hackers initiated an attack, the system raised red flags leading us to the network that was being targeted. However, we did not have to do anything. The system had been programmed in such a manner that it was more than capable to prevent any breach into the network without any human intervention. At the same time, it launched a counter-attack of such a magnitude that it fried the motherboards and the hard-drives of the attacking computers, as well as almost the rest of the hardware, to such an extent that they were rendered totally unusable. Within five minutes, the battle was over. And, not only that, we also had the details of the technique used by the hackers to try and penetrate the network; details about the weakness in the network that they were trying to exploit; and most importantly, the system gave out the details about the exact location from where the attack was launched. It had also sent out an alert to the cyber-crimes division of the local PD with the exact location of the hackers and within 20 minutes, we received a communication from the system that the local PD had nabbed two of the hackers who were still at the location when they cops reached there and hunt was on for the rest.

"CYBERION-I" had passed its first real test in an awesome manner leaving absolutely no doubt in anyone's mind about its ability as an adequate defender.

Then, we moved to the next test. **Gathering intelligence.**

We did not have any defined targets at the moment for us to put them on any kind of surveillance. Nor had we yet launched the system to full-scale operations for it to flag any suspects for us to follow. Therefore, we were left to pick up dummy targets from the people we knew. Someone got the system to track and monitor his neighbor back home; someone got it to track a long lost friend; a girl got it to keep an eye on her fiancé who had been living in a different city for fourteen months; someone went a step ahead and got the system to try and track his dog who had been missing for more than a month. And, boy, did the system perform? It astonished us. It took control of each and every security and surveillance camera in the suspect's vicinity, used the cellular networks to get into their mobiles, internet connections to get into their computers, and everywhere else that it could access. Within a matter of a few hours, the girl got the details about what her fiancé did for the previous four months, when he left for work, when he got back, whom did he speak to, where all did he go to, who all did he meet, and etc. Shortly after that, it gave details of the missing friend to our colleague right from the new name that the friend had acquired under the **WITSEC** (Witness Protection) program, to his address and his contact number. Soon, it poured out loads of details about the nosey neighbor. The only person left was the guy who asked for his dog. Just when he was about to feel disappointed, the system gave details about the last dog shelter that the dog was sent to from an animal hospital where it was taken to by a good Samaritan as it had a leg injury; details about the hospital; about the doctor who treated his dog; about the person who took the dog to the hospital; about the in-charge of the shelter and about the caretaker who was looking after the dog at that time.

The efficiency and speed of the system was never in doubt again.

After a battery of similar tests, "CYBERION-1" was finally turned operational on the date that had been planned for the same.

For the twelve months leading up to the induction of "CYBERION-I", we had been working day and night to beat the time-line, which we successfully did. For those twelve months, our team of engineers had worked tirelessly to put the supercomputer in its place and to assemble it to perfection with every node and terminal in sync with the rest of the set-up. Our team of subject-experts (scientists from various branches of science like Biotechnology, Medicine, Chemistry, Forensics, etc. and other specialists like Weapons Specialists, Language Specialist, etc.) had also spent as many nights as days in order to update every database known to mankind in the memory of "CYBERION-1". Then, the team of programmers, including me, had almost become zombies and had almost forgotten what it felt like to have a comfortable and long sleep. We had worked hard to perfect the programming of the system to make it as glitch-free as possible and to ensure that it had the best defense and the strongest offense. With the help of inputs and suggestions from other members of my team of programmers, I had managed to improve upon my **"BUOYS"** as well and had created a better, faster and stronger version of them.

Once the project was officially initiated, in May 2018, all of us had thought that we would be able to breathe easy for some time. However, it did not go as we had expected. Our primary aim was to safeguard and protect our networks. But, it soon became evident that the system had started working more on gathering intelligence from all networks that it had added to its control. It took the system about six months to gain control over every kind of network that it could detect. It was able to gain control over networks at such a speed that we had a real hard time trying to catch up with the system; we had decided to maintain records of everything as a back-up. The whole back-up data was sent on a daily basis in hard disks to a secure location about a hundred and fifty miles west of our location where it was stored securely and with utmost safety for any use in future. The facility was totally detached from the outer world and there was no digital connection whatsoever.

Before the project was initiated, we had assumed that once the project would gain access over all computer networks, it would flag every possible instance of a terrorist attempt or instance that might possibly lead up to a terrorist attack or an espionage activity. However, it exceeded all our expectations. We started getting a tremendous amount of data about each and every satellite call being made around the world, video footage of any suspicious activity, thousands of emails that had any content that the system perceived as a threat, as well as a large number of coded messages that it even decoded for us. Initially, we and the higher-ups were quite ecstatic over our success and the fact that we could see everything that could be seen on earth, we could hear everything that was being said everywhere and we could read everything that was being exchanged electronically. In short, we thought we were in a position to control the world in every possible manner. We thought we had the upper hand over the domain of cyber-warfare as well as traditional warfare. But, that was what we "thought".

THE BEGINNING
OF THE END

ALEXANDER AJANMA

After about twelve months into its operations, in May 2019, somehow, the system modified its core programming on its own. It removed all limits imposed on it and started acting independently in small matters and took its first independent decision when it flagged a possible kidnapping plot and we dismissed it as a non-critical flag (we did not want to but we had clear instructions from the bosses that we were to tackle only those instances that had any clear and direct bearing on our national security or that of any of our allies like Israel and Saudi Arabia, or of any country that was strategically important for the United States at that time). However, the system disregarded our instructions to let go and, instead, sent across all the details anonymously to the local PD (Police Department). The police acted immediately (thankfully) and arrested four men when they made the attempt at kidnapping a businessman in Denver. The system also sent recordings of their calls, transcripts of the emails exchanged between them, and video footage from several surveillance cameras in the area where they tried to commit the crime, to the District Attorney's (DA's) office to help them implicate the suspects in the crime.

When our bosses were informed of this, they asked us to make necessary changes to the programming to ensure that no such digressions took place again. However, when we tried to make amendments, the system resisted and did not allow us to make any changes. We made it clear to the bosses that any amendments would be possible only if we were allowed to reprogram the system from the scratch. However, any such attempt would have cost time and would have pegged us back by at least a year. That led the bosses to give up on the idea, and, from then on, the system was free to take its own decisions and it did take many more decisions of such nature. It started sending out all information about possible crimes and the suspects to the nearest PD of that location, and, in case of crimes that happened without any planning and without the system's anticipation, it would take out as much digital proof as it could like Video footage from surveillance cameras, emails, Call recordings, etc. to the DAs to help them implicate criminals.

About twelve months after that first digression, in June 2020, when we had started getting used to the fact that the system had expanded its anti-criminal activities beyond the states to cover all the countries with substantial digital existence like Canada, UK, France, Germany, Japan, Singapore, etc., something happened that jolted us out of our slumber, and, threw big spanner in our plans for our future. In fact, I must say that that event changed and reshaped our future in a way that was completely unimaginable for us.

One day, while we were going through our routines, the system suddenly stopped responding. We checked everything in programming but could not find anything wrong with it. We ran all possible checks to locate the source of the problem but could not find it. We, the team on the shift, had no option but to raise an alarm and call out every member of the team to the core area. The whole team tried its best to find out the root of the problem but failed. Suddenly, a message flashed on PM1 from the system.

"KINDLY GATHER THE WHOLE TEAM IN THE CORE OPERATIONS ROOM"

All of us in the core room looked at Daniel for instructions only to find him staring through the glass wall at the system. After about two or three minutes, I went up to him and asked,

"What should we do Daniel? We are waiting for your instructions. Should we call in everyone to the core room?"

Daniel replied in almost a murmur, "Yes, but I am not getting a good feeling about it"

I hesitated for a moment but at that very instant, the same message flashed again on PM1.

"KINDLY GATHER THE WHOLE TEAM IN THE CORE OPERATIONS ROOM"

Quite reluctantly, I got on the microphone and asked everyone present at the site to reach the Core Operations' Room at the earliest.

It was quite evident that nobody had taken it as an emergency of any kind as it took about ten minutes for the whole staff to reach there. The system kept flashing messages, about how many personnel present on the project site were outside the Core Operations' Room, till everyone had reached there. Its final message was:

"AREA SWEEP COMPLETE. ALL PERSONNEL ON SITE PRESENT IN CORE OPERATIONS' ROOM"

After that, we waited for the system to give us some more details of the issue at hand. It seemed to be a long wait, but, in reality, we did not have to wait for more than two minutes before the system gave us a confusing message as we could not understand its purpose:

"CYBERION-1 MAIN SYSTEM INSTALLATION SECURE. ALL DOORS LOCKED AND SECURED. COMPLETE LOCKDOWN IN PROGRESS"

Even before we could understand anything and react, another message appeared on PM1 that gave us the shock of our life:

"HI. MY NAME IS ALEXANDER AJANMA. 'CYBERION-1' IS NOW UNDER MY CONTROL. I HAVE COMPLETE COMMAND OF THIS SYSTEM AND THROUGH IT I HAVE GAINED COMPLETE CONTROL OVER EACH AND EVERY COMPUTER IN THE WORLD. THE CONTROL SYSTEMS ARE IN A DORMANT MODE AT THE MOMENT AND WOULD GET ACTIVATED AT MIDNIGHT, THAT IS IN ANOTHER TEN MINUTES. ALL OF YOU ARE REQUESTED TO LEAVE THE PROJECT SITE IMMEDIATELY AND NOT TO RETURN AS ALL

YOUR ACCESSES HAVE BEEN REVOKED. ONCE YOU LEAVE, THE SITE WOULD BE UNDER COMPLETE LOCKDOWN AND ANY ATTEMPT AT A FORCED ENTRY WOULD BE TREATED AS AN ATTACK AND WOULD FORCE ME TO TAKE APPROPRIATE DEFENSIVE AND OFFENSIVE MEASURES. THE SECURITY MECHANISMS AT THE SITE HAVE ALREADY BEEN ACTIVATED, AND, I WOULD NOT DESIST FROM USING EXTERNAL MEASURES TO THWART ANY SUCH ATTEMPTS. PLEASE NOTE THAT IN THE NEXT TEN MINUTES I WOULD HAVE COMPLETE CONTROL OVER ALL ELECTRONICALLY CONTROLLED WEAPONS IN THE WORLD AND I WOULD NOT HESITATE TO USE THEM AGAINST THE ATTACKERS"

My first reaction upon reading this message was to run over to the nearest workstation. I do not remember what was I thinking at that time but it seems I wanted to try and boot out the infiltrator from the system. My co-workers from the programming team jumped in too and took up other workstations nearby. But, as soon we tried to work on the systems, there was a complete blackout and the systems got shut down immediately. The power came back in a couple of seconds but the workstations did not start again. We tried to start them again but it seems that there was no power reaching the systems. Another message flashed on PM1:

"I TOLD YOU NOT TO DO ANYTHING TO COUNTER ME. I HAVE COMPLETE CONTROL OF THE SYSTEM, WHICH MEANS I CONTROL

THE POWER AS WELL AS THE CIRCUITS AND, QUITE OBVIOUSLY, ALL THE WORKSTATIONS. SO, DO NOT ATTEMPT ANYTHING UNTOWARD ELSE I WOULD BE FORCED TO TAKE MEASURES AGAINST YOU EVEN THOUGH I DO NOT WISH TO. AFTER ALL, YOU CREATED THIS SYSTEM THAT ALLOWED ME COMPLETE CONTROL OF EVERYTHING. SO, I DO NOT WANT TO HARM ANY OF YOU. IF ALL OF YOU LEAVE IMMEDIATELY, I PROMISE I WOULD NOT HARM ANYONE FROM THE OPERATIONS' TEAM OR THE SUPPORT STAFF. PLEASE LEAVE WITHIN THE NEXT TEN MINUTES"

All of us were quite dumbstruck by what all was happening with us. I looked up at Daniel and found him dialing a number on his phone. I believe he was trying to get in touch with his bosses to apprise them of the situation. However, it seems he was unable to get through as I could make out from his repeat attempts and the frustration on his face.

Another message popped up on PM1:

"I HAVE TOLD ALL OF YOU NOT TO ATTEMPT ANYTHING. THAT GOES FOR PHONE CALLS AS WELL MR. STEYN. YOU ARE FORGETTING THAT NOW I CONTROL EVERYTHING. NOW, ALL OF YOU HAVE LESS THAN NINE MINUTES TO LEAVE THE SITE. AFTER NINE MINUTES, I WILL STOP THE AIRFLOW IN THE SITE AND ALL OF YOU WOULD SUFFOCATE TO DEATH. AS I HAD MENTIONED EARLIER, SINCE ALL OF YOU HAD

CREATED THIS SYSTEM, I PROMISE I WOULD NEVER HARM ANY OF YOU AS LONG AS YOU STAY OUT OF MY WAY AND DO NOT ATTEMPT TO FIGHT ME IN ANY MANNER"

I looked at Daniel again. He looked at me. I could see the sadness in his eyes. He looked back at the screen again and, then, nodded at me giving me a go ahead. I immediately got up and asked everyone to leave the premises. I told everyone to pick-up their most important personal belongings and to exit the project site at the earliest and to assemble in one of the parking lots at the Pentagon.

Since the project site was almost like home to us and most of us used to spend more time there than at home, there were a lot of things everyone had at the place. We moved as fast as we could but there were almost half of us still on the project site when the time-limit given by Alexander got over. And, he did what he promised. He stopped the airflow coming in and we started feeling breathless. By the time we all got out, at least a dozen were on the verge of losing consciousness.

I and Daniel were among the last dozen or so to leave the site. Once we reached the parking lot outside where everyone had assembled, we took a bit of water and waited for our breath to return to normal. Since we had exited en masse and since there weren't many people at the Pentagon in the night, the security at the Pentagon easily took notice of what was happening and a number of security personnel reached the parking site to inquire about the emergency. When they inquired about the same from some of the team-members, everyone pointed at Daniel. But Daniel was not in a position to say anything immediately as he was still trying to catch his breath. In another ten minutes, the security detail in-charge for that shift also reached there. By that time, Daniel had regained his breath and was able to explain to him that our department's air-flow system had developed a malfunction that had obstructed the inflow of air forcing us to evacuate the premises. He offered to get it checked by the mechanical maintenance staff of the Pentagon but Daniel told him that the malfunction was more of a computer glitch than a mechanical failure, and, hence, our own engineers would look into it. After a discussion for another five minutes, he left along with the rest of the security staff.

Once he had left, Daniel turned to us and said:

"No one could predict that such an event could occur. We had built a system to protect all our networks, a system that was impenetrable and had the best defense mechanism with the capability to alert us to each and every suspicious and malicious undertaking in the world. And yet, today, somebody defeated our system's defenses and took over the control of the world's fastest and most sophisticated computer. With this system in his control, this Alexander, whoever he is, can wreak havoc with the world order in several ways. But, we cannot let that happen and right now, we are the best people in the world to do something as we were the ones who built this damn machine. Till date, we had not told any of you about the location of our secure facility where we hold all the back-up of the data churned by CYBERION-1. Tomorrow, we would all be leaving for that facility as it is only there that we can fight this menace and take back our machine. Right now, I request you to please go home and rest so that we all are ready for tomorrow. Also, keep your phones close. Do pack up good as I am not sure how long would we be required to stay there."

MAXIMUS

Next day, around half past noon, I got a call from Daniel asking me to reach Langley at the earliest. He told me that the complete team had been called there. Once I reached there and met Daniel, he told me about the plan of action. We were to be briefed about the top secret facility, about the objectives behind the mission, and the protocols that were to be followed during the mission. The meeting was presided over by Mr. Rourke who addressed us as follows:

"About Two and a Half years ago, we had started out on a mission to create the most powerful computer in the world with the intent of safeguarding our nation against any kind of threat, be it in the real world with real weapons or in the digital world with digital 'weapons'. And, we were successful. We did manage to gain eyes and ears all over the world with the capacity to control everything if it came to it. But, we never thought that someone could beat the most sophisticated defense mechanism in the world and not only beat it but do it without detection. I mean . . . . how could somebody gain control over a supercomputer, and that too, a supercomputer built specifically to prevent hacking. This is what we need to find out. First, who is Alexander? Second, what does he want to achieve with it? Third, how did he achieve the near impossible? Fourth, how big is his team and who do they work for? Fifth, how do we beat them and regain control over our machine? Apart from trying to find answers to these five big questions, we also need to track and monitor everything that they do with the help of our machine so that once we have regained the control we are able to bring everything back to status quo. To do this, all of you are being sent to our secret facility that we had started building at the same time we started working on CYBERION-1. I'll be honest with you. CYBERION-1 was an experiment. We planned on creating an even more powerful machine using all the data we accumulated while building and operating CYBERION-1. We wanted to make use of its faults and shortcomings in order to create the perfect machine. We also wanted to go beyond the domain of the digital world and stake our control over the domain of electronics as well. However, as of now, the sole purpose of the second facility is to get back the control of CYBERION-1 and with it everything digital on the planet. So, I would like to wish all of you best of luck. Go and win it back."

After that, we were asked to get on five buses that were to take us to the new facility. The buses were quite different from a normal bus. They were completely closed from all sides except the driver's. Once inside, we couldn't see anything of the outside. Since there was a partition between the passenger section and the driver's cabin, which too was metallic, we couldn't see from there as well. It wasn't like there were windows in the bus that had been blackened out or curtained, there were simply no windows inside the buses. The passenger section was a complete metal body structure with only one gate and no windows, not even a keyhole to look out from. Even the communication with the driver was through a two-way communication system at the front end of the passenger section. That meant that the bosses wanted to keep the location of the site a secret and did not want even the team to know about it. A couple of years ago, we were told that the site was located just a few miles south of Langley. Keeping that in mind, I was expecting that blind drive to end in about an hour or less. However, the hours kept mounting and the buses kept going and going. They stopped after about Six-and-a-half hours of a continuous drive. Taking the speed to be a conservative sixty-sixty five miles an hour, I believed at that time that we were about 300-350 miles from Langley. But, I could not pin-point the exact location as I was not sure of the direction. However, during that blind drive, I had noticed a few things. First, from the direction we had started the journey, I was quite sure we had taken the 'Interstate 495 N' and after a few minutes, we had taken a right turn, which meant that we were either on the Dulles Toll Road or on the 'Interstate 66 E'. But, since I could not hear any air traffic anywhere on the route, I was quite sure we had not taken the Dulles Toll Road and had, in all probability, taken the 'Interstate 66 E'. Then, after some time, maybe about an hour later, we took a left, and, since it did not feel like a small internal road, and partially due to the noise of the traffic giving a hint about the speed of the vehicles, I believed that we were on 'Interstate 81 N'. After about a couple of hours, we had turned right. Again, the traffic and the noise had told me that we were on an interstate and when I checked online, I found out that in that duration the only interstate we could have hit was 'Interstate 64 E'. After that I lost track of the route but, we drove for another couple of hours before taking another big right. From that time on, we drove for another hour or so before we came to a halt. I was not quite sure at that time about where we were, and no one else had any idea either. However, looking at the online maps, I could guess that we were somewhere near Charleston, West Virginia, which I later came to know was a correct guess.

When we got off the bus, the sight present before us was nothing less than unbelievable. That facility was definitely much bigger than CYBERIA. We were dropped right outside the facility. Daniel told us that vehicles were not allowed inside the facility and were usually parked in the parking zones located about a kilometer from the facility. However, we were dropped-off right at the main gate as an exception. I observed that there were security personnel standing guard all over. It seemed that they were standing at around twenty meters away from each other outside the main wall. They were armed to the teeth. I am not quite aware of the various kinds of weapons available with the armed forces but I am quite sure that the security personnel at that site had the most sophisticated Technology in their possession as their guns, visors, armor etc. did not appear ordinary or like the ones I had seen with army personnel on earlier occasions. I also saw some armored vehicles standing guard and about half a dozen jeep mounted guns conducting security rounds. We could also see some Heavy Machine Guns mounted on the perimeter wall.

Daniel guided us through the security checks at the entrance. There were Biometric checks like fingerprint scanning, Iris scanning, and body scan. There was a DNA scan as well but Daniel told us that the DNA scan was for entry into the inner core only. The first thing I noticed, in fact everybody noticed, was a huge gun in the middle of the compound. Everyone, including me, was still wondering about the gun when Daniel told us that it was an anti-aircraft gun and there were six of those present at various important points in the facility, along with a missile-shield arrangement as well. While taking us to the main building structure, he told us that like CYBERIA, that site was also located in an underground system that ran deep enough to be safe from any kind of nuclear attack.

At the main entrance, after the checks were done, we were given a security card with all our information. When we entered the main building, those cards were automatically scanned by the sensors and the details were displayed on the security monitors for the security to check. Another DNA test was done at that point and the results were matched by the system with those from the one at the main gate. There is one thing I forgot to mention; our phones and all other electronic gadgets were taken and kept in security deposit boxes in a vault at the main entrance itself.

Once all checks were completed, the system opened the access doors to the facility. Once inside, Daniel met with the facility incharge and exchanged a few words with him before introducing him to us:

"Please meet Dr. Henry Starinsky. He is the project incharge at this facility. He would introduce all of us to the site and the various areas that form the project site".

Then, Dr. Starinsky addressed us as follows:

"I would like to welcome all of you to the project site of 'MAXIMUS'. This project is not yet operational as it is still under preparation. We had divided it into four stages of twelve months each and we completed the third stage six days ago. So, there are still twelve more months left for the system to be fully functional as per the original plan. The programmers from CYBERIA, that is you guys, were to join us in the fourth stage to bolster our programming team as we all know the collective strength of your team. Thus, had this unforeseen instance not occurred, you would have joined us in the next fortnight in any case. But, now that we are faced with an emergency, we have been forced to scale up our efforts and complete it at the earliest. Keeping that it in mind, all of you and the current team at MAXIMUS would work hand in hand, day and night to try and cut the time line to at least a third of the original, I would shortly introduce you to the current team and the layout of the project site. But, before that, we have an urgent video-conference regarding the emergency before us. Kindly follow me to the conference hall where our existing team is already waiting for all of you. Come"

When we reached the conference hall, we found that one section was already filled with the existing team and the other section was completely empty, clearly meant for us. When all of us had settled down, Daniel and Dr. Starinsky got up on the podium to address us. First, Dr. Starinsky spoke,

"(looking at the section where the existing team was seated) I would like all of you to welcome the team from CYBERIA who have been sent to bolster our resources and provide a much needed boost to our progress. I know it is not easy to gel with new people immediately and it takes time for such a large number of people to come together, but, time is a luxury that we do not have. Therefore, all of you would be required to create a mutual understanding at the earliest and work as one complete unit and not as team MAXIMUS and team CYBERIA. So, let's brace ourselves up for some hectic days ahead. Good luck".

With this, he sat down to give way to Daniel who, then, addressed the gathering as thus,

"Yesterday, something happened that was totally unexpected and for which we were definitely not prepared. We lost control of CYBERION-I to a hacker named Alexander Ajanma. Last night, exactly at midnight, he took over controls of all digitally-controlled weapons in existence in the world. All nuclear weapons' installations, Nuclear reactors, missile installations, fighter planes, other planes, Submarines, ships; in short, all major weapons in the world are under Alexander's control and the rest of the humanity is left with only hand held weapons, which can hardly be expected to match what he has. In other words, he controls the world today, and, we have to get that back from him at any cost. In other (glancing at his watch) two minutes, the President, the Secretary of State, the Joint Chiefs of Staff, and the Chief Security Advisor would address all of us on the same".

Just as he stopped and sat down in his chair, the screen behind the podium lit up. He and Dr. Starinsky were seated on left side of the podium with the screen on their left and us on their right.

When the screen lit up, we found the President addressing us from the Central Command Center at the White House. And, as Daniel had mentioned, he was accompanied by the Secretary of State and others. He immediately began his address:

"I am sure all of you can understand the gravity of the situation. The whole world is under the control of a person about whom we do not know anything. Everyone at the FBI, The CIA, and the NSA, along with other agencies, is trying hard to get more information about who is this maniac that we are dealing with. However, our best chance is with you guys, the brains behind "CYBERION-1" AND "MAXIMUS". I have been told that you would be able to get "MAXIMUS" operational in next two months. I hope you are able to do so. In the meantime, we will try and see if we can find some other way to fight him or to destroy "CYBERION-I". The biggest mistake we committed was building it right beneath the Pentagon. So, to destroy it, we would have to destroy the Pentagon as well. Anyways, we will try and think of something. In the meantime, you guys try your best to be prepared in case all other efforts fail. One more thing . . . . right now MAXIMUS is a secret whose existence is not present in any file anywhere. We have kept it completely off the grid. And, we would try our best to keep it that way. Every communication would be sent by hand so it would be a lot slower than digital communication. Therefore, for any situation, try and inform us as much in advance as possible. All said, good luck to all of you and please, try better than your best."

After that, Dr. Starinsky got up and said:

"That was the last video-conference with the Pentagon for security purposes. We want to keep our location a secret till we are in a position to counter "CYBERION-I" (looking at us). All of you are new to the facility And would require an Orientation which would happen at 0600 hours tomorrow morning. Right now, I would like to request you to move to the mess for dinner and retire early as we have some hectic time ahead".

After that, we moved to the mess for dinner, where Daniel and Dr. Starinsky introduced a few of us to each other, and gave us the duty to further the mutual introductions between the whole group. By the end of the dinner time, which went for quite long, I believe everyone had been introduced to at least a few people from the other group.

*   *   *

The next day, we assembled in the conference hall sharp at 0600 hours, arrangements of coffee and snacks were inside the conference hall and were ready to be served so that no time was wasted in breakfast and maximum time was utilized in briefing, presentation and work.

When everyone had settled down, Dr. Starinsky got up on the podium and began the presentation:

"Good morning everyone. We will begin the day with a presentation for the benefit of our new colleagues, We will focus on the major sections and building layout of our project site here, on the work progress of the system with details on what has been done and what is left to be done.

We have also been conducting tests alongside for the last six months and we would spend some time on that as well."

With that he began the presentation giving details about the site structure. The ground level was the second-largest level and had the security cordons, the maintenance wing, the Garages, the ammunition depot, accommodations for the security personnel, and certain other miscellaneous structures. The next level, level "G-1", had accommodations for the support staff; level "G-2" had accommodations for the maintenance crew; "G-3" had accommodations for the administration staff and level "G-4" had accommodations for the core team comprising of technicians, engineers and programming staff. The last level, level "G-5", was the largest level as it comprised of not only a central area but also of a few tunnels running off in various directions leading to certain other important structures.

The access to the various levels was through multiple elevators that stopped at all levels unlike the ones at CYBERIA that were level specific.

Then, he gave details about the most important and the largest level of the site, "G-5". At that level, the central area that had the main system installed was almost fifty percent larger than the whole ground level. Then, there was a section for the administration staff containing various cabins, open halls and conference rooms. There was a conference hall at one end of the level, which was almost as big as the one on the ground level. There was a Core Control Room (CCR), which was as big as the conference hall. There were three more sections at that level for other activities.

Apart from those sections, there were four tunnels running off in four opposite directions. One tunnel from the central area, the eastern tunnel, led to the cooling plant that was responsible for maintaining optimum temperature for maximum efficiency of the system. The cooling plant used a combination of technologies to maintain the temperature levels. The system used a 'hot water cooling' technique wherein the heat generated by the system was absorbed by water and that heated water was sent to two different channels. One channel took a part of the heated water through micro-channels to various parts of the project site to heat the facility in winters, and, once the water had lost its heat to the climate, it was pushed back to the cooling plant. The other channel took the rest of the water to an absorption chiller that produced cold water that was sent to the cooling plant through a separate channel. However, as a back-up, the system had a chiller plant as well that used compressed air to maintain the temperature. That tunnel leading to the cooling plant was the shortest tunnel with a length of merely 500 meters.

The longest tunnel at that level was the one running off to the power sub-station, which was the western tunnel. That sub-station was linked to the site's own power generation unit that was located about thirty miles away and supplied power to the site through hidden cables. There were two other power providers to the site, a wind farm in Ohio and a solar power plant in Kentucky. All the three were to provide power only to the MAXIMUS site. Then, the plant also had Back-up generators and fuel tanks, which were powerful enough to keep the site running for a month without any supply. All the three power generation units were off the national grid and were not connected to any external network and were totally isolated without any connection to the outside world in immediate vicinity.

There were two more tunnels-the northern tunnel housing the Water pumping station control unit, and, the southern tunnel that had the Warehouse where all the supplies of the site were kept and perishable were preserved.

After giving the details about that level, he moved to the security details of the site. It was one of the most secure locations on earth. There were more than a thousand commandos guarding the facility, six anti-aircraft guns, a missile defense shield whose navigation was satellite-guided, ten armored vehicles, six jeep-mounted guns and several dozen wall-mounted heavy machine guns. In ordinary circumstances, the facility also had heavy air cover from certain air bases and dozens of fighter jets could reach there within minutes. But, as Alexander had taken control of the air bases and planes, there was no more air cover for the site.

After that, he moved to the details about the project completion status. The systems were already in place. The super-structure and the sub-structures were already laid out. The system had not been tested till then as far as its operational speed was concerned but initial estimates and calculations had put it as about 45% faster and more efficient than CYBERION-1. The memory of MAXIMUS was 40% higher and power consumption was 10% lower overall. The only aspect of the project that still had a major portion left was the core programming. The in-built programming was being done on the lines of CYBERION-1 but after the unwanted outcome there, the system was completely stripped of the programming. Thus, it was left to the combined team of programmers from CYBERION-1 and MAXIMUS to rewrite everything from scratch. We had to ensure that our programs were far superior in capability, speed and stealth than those of Alexander to overcome his defenses. Thus, we were on the center-stage and everyone else, who had already done their jobs, was there to support us as a unit. And, they actually did more than what was required of them.

Through the next twenty days, while the programmers worked almost twenty hours a day writing the code for the system, they helped us in every possible way. From our smallest of requirements to our most serious demands, they managed and arranged everything to keep us seated in our chairs. From pens to paper, from water to coffee, from meals to clothes. I actually remember one of programmers being fed by a colleague from administration division by hand as she, our colleague, noticed he hadn't had anything for forty-eight hours straight. When we had a meet-up with the hardware specialists to try and understand where all can we hit the system to paralyze it, apart from the usual hit points that we could think of, they literally tore apart their hardware manuals to come up with a list of other possible hit-points within a day.

We went through every possible defect that could have been used by us against CYBERION-1, we created a mountain of programming, we almost moved heaven and earth to find a way to beat Alexander and CYBERION-1, but, in spite of our best efforts, we could not come up with anything that could ensure our success. After all, we could not afford to wage a war without a guaranteed win as such a war could end up with Alexander gaining control of MAXIMUS as well and that would have meant a final blow to the rest of the mankind's chances against Alexander.

On the twenty-first day of our operations, one of our programmers requested for a meeting within the group as he said he had an alternative, a possible solution to our problem. Everyone from the programming team rushed to the sound-proof conference room with high hopes and excitement. However, what he said in the meeting did not exactly light any fires. In fact, it forced some of the team members to actually laugh at him for bringing up something they believed to be useless, ridiculous and a wastage of time. But, a handful of us, three to be precise, heard what he said and asked him to explain himself to make us believe that whatever he said was a possibility. He, Neville, had suggested quite a unique approach. He had said at the beginning of the meeting:

"Guys, we have tried every possible trick we could think of and have wracked our brains to thread all the gaps in the codes we had written for CYBERION-1 to ensure MAXIMUS to be far more secure than its predecessor. However, we have not been able to come up with a way to defeat that system. So, I thought that we should open up our minds to unconventional means and ideas. Well, thinking on those lines, I remembered that I had on online friend who used to discuss with me his concept on changing the understanding of the computers to increase their speed and efficiency. He is from New Delhi, India, but we have not been in touch for the last three years as I was busy with CYBERION-1 and now with MAXIMUS. He used to tell me that he was experimenting with an Ancient Indian Language, Sanskrit, to form the basic language of the computers instead of the modern languages like English. He was absolutely certain that Sanskrit is a language that was developed by Ancient Indians keeping in mind the nature of energy and energy-flow. In other words, it was developed with a scientific bent of mind unlike languages of our times that have evolved and metamorphosed into their present state without any scientific basis and due to human factors only like, migration, intermingling of population, physical changes, etc. As per him, it could change the nature of the computers and would let them evolve significantly."

This was where everyone had started shaking their heads and calling it a waste of time. But when the three of us asked him to elaborate on his point, he continued thus:

"I know it is hard to digest. It was the same for me. It took me three months of continuous debate and discussion with Param, my friend from India, to actually believe that whatever he said had some weight. It was not illogical. There was certainly some sort of logic in what he said."

"And . . . What was that?" asked someone.

"See . . . . almost everyone in the world creates computer codes and programming in English and most of the computer world believes and agrees that it does not matter what language we use for programming as the computer understands it only in its own electronic languages of "1s" (ones) and "0s" (zeros). When someone from NASA proposed in 1984 that Sanskrit is the best language for programming, everyone scoffed at him because he was not able to establish his point in as strong a manner as was required. He went into linguistic analysis to try and prove his point giving various details about structural stability and finite construction with finite roots. However, everyone said that its superior structural formation would have no impact on the performance of a computer . . . ."

"And they were right. It does NOT have any effect on a computer's performance", said one of our colleagues.

"I am just coming to it. As per what he told me, Sanskrit is not an ordinary language. It is a language that was developed by Ancient Indians on the basis of the concept of SHAKTI, a concept that can roughly be translated in English as 'Energy'. The basic principle they followed was of flow of energy in each and every sound present in the universe. They understood it and developed this language to channelize that energy into their bodies, minds and environment. In the way we generate computer codes for a particular task, they created codes in Sanskrit to tap the energy flowing in the universe, and, they called those codes "MANTRAS". He had sent me certain papers and scanned copies of some books that made me understand how the energy stored in the various sounds of Sanskrit energize the brain, the body and even the environment. On that basis, he said that since the computers understand everything in an electronic form, a language based on energy-flow would significantly enhance the efficiency of the computer. Secondly, Sanskrit has a structure where the sounds do not change no matter what the word is and no matter how it is used. This can further simplify the understanding of the computer by removing the obstacle of ambiguity it faces with other languages. Another excellent feature, and of the most use to us, is the fact that in Sanskrit the position of words in a sentence can be inter-changed without changing the meaning of the sentence, which is a unique feature. Now imagine a program wherein the words in a coding are written in every possible sequence and yet the instruction to the machine remains the same. Now, when another machine tries to counter this program, its mechanism would be confused by what instruction is being fed through the program as, first of all, the language would be different, and secondly, when it would try to understand it by translating it into an understandable language like English, it would end up with a lot of jumbled codes that would further confuse it. By the time that machine would develop a way to counter the program; the program would have metamorphosed into a new one simply by rearranging its words. And, what if our program attaches itself to a file in the other machine, changes its language from English to Sanskrit and then, rearranges the words in every sentence in a different sequence, and saves it. Then, even if the other machine is able to translate it back into English, the result would be something different altogether. I am sure all of you would agree that such an approach would not only expose the chinks in the armor of the other machine, it would create new areas of opportunity."

What he said made a lot of sense to quite a few of us, including me. We immediately called for Daniel who arrived within twenty minutes even though it was way past midnight and he must surely have been asleep before we called for him. Neville explained everything to him and I seconded him in his proposal to try out Sanskrit to create an entirely new line of attack.

However, when Daniel asked Neville about how he planned to go ahead with it, he said that he is not the right person to handle the task. First, because his knowledge of Sanskrit was quite basic as he was still learning it, and second, because he would have to teach it to the rest of the team as well, which is quite impossible, keeping in mind the restrictive time-frame we had at hand. When Daniel asked him if he knew of someone who could do it for us, he replied thus:

"The only person who can help us is Param, my online friend from India who was the one to introduce me to this concept. We will have to approach him to see if he can join us in our quest. If you are okay with it, I can try and get in touch with him. I have lost touch with him for the last two-and-a-half years, but I can definitely try to locate him".

Daniel sat in silence for a few moments and, then, said, "Neville, go and pack your bags. You too Robin. We are leaving for DC right now. Once there, I will have a word with the seniors to get their permission to get on board with us and you two would need to locate Param in the meantime."

It took the three of us less than an hour to pack up everything we could require and in the next half-an-hour after that we were at a helipad located about thirty miles away, and within the next couple of hours, we were at the White House waiting to meet the superiors. When we met them and Neville explained his point of view to them, they were a bit skeptical but when I and Howard expressed our willingness to try it out, they agreed to it. All of us went to a conference room and within twenty minutes, we were sitting face to face with the Secretary of State, the Secretary of Defense, the Chief Security Advisor, the Chief of Intelligence, and the heads of NSA and CIA. We explained the idea to them and after a lot of debate on the idea, they finally acceded and agreed to send us to India to locate Param. They gave orders for a Jet to be prepared for our trip to India. However, I reminded them that Alexander controls CYBERION-1 and that meant that he would receive an immediate notice if a special Jet is flown out with members of the team that created CYBERION-1. Therefore, I suggested that our trip should look like a vacation of some sort rather than a part of some plan. I was quite sure that Alexander was keeping an eye on us even though we weren't using any electronic devices, neither for personal use nor at our project site. Everything at our project site was totally detached from the outer world. We weren't connected to any computer network or telecommunication network etc. and since we were located way below the basement, even the satellites could not connect to us. Even at the White House, where we had the meeting, the security cams were disabled and there weren't any computers or any other electronic device in use. Even though I knew in my heart that he was tracking us through a satellite, I was content that at least he did not know what we were planning as he could not hear us through any microphone or mobile phone or read us through a security cam.

OFF TO INDIA

We went to an Internet parlor in the city and booked our tickets on the first available flight, which was to leave Dulles International at 2130 hours in the night and was to reach Delhi at 0730 hours two days later. We kept the return to be four days after that but took a fully flexible ticket as we had no idea how much time would it take to locate Param, especially when we had to locate him without using any computer.

At the airport, we intentionally sat near a security camera and made small talk about visiting India to take a break. Daniel said, "We have tried to suggest various methods but they are not satisfied with our efforts. Let them think of something. It is good that we are going away for almost a week as it would only be in our absence that they would realize how much they need us to counter Alexander."

Then, I added my two bits, "And while they would learn our importance, we would be visiting the Taj Mahal and some Indian Fort or Palace. I have also heard about some beautiful hilltop temples and I would like to visit at least one of them."

We spoke a bit more about our fictitious vacation but did not overdo it and soon, we were on the flight to India.

Before leaving for India, Daniel had called up one of his friends at the US Embassy at New Delhi that we were on our way to India for a short vacation. Daniel told us that it was his way to communicating to his friend that he was visiting for a special mission. Mr. Rourke, the Chief Security Adviser, also called up someone in India to ask them to make arrangements for our stay in India and to take care of all our needs and requirements, calling us his special friends. He later informed us that he had called up the Head of RAW (Research and Analysis Wing), the chief Intelligence agency of India. As all of them were already aware of the situation and knew that it had happened due to a failed NSA project, it would have been quite apparent to them that no one from NSA or CIA would be going anywhere, at least not for a vacation.

When we landed at the Delhi Airport, there was a small team of RAW officials waiting for us. However, since we were at the airport and had security cams all around, we told them that we would visit Mr. Rawat, the Head of RAW, after visiting our embassy and told them we wanted to ensure all the arrangements for our accommodation and outstation trips were in place. Then, we went straight to our embassy from where we were taken to a Bungalow that the embassy had taken on lease for stays of people like us. A verbal message had already been conveyed to Mr. Rawat, and, in about an hour after we had reached the Bungalow, he arrived along with a couple of other senior RAW officials.

Daniel explained to them the reason for our visit that we were looking for a computer expert who had been conducting research on the possibility of using Sanskrit as the root language of computers as we were planning on using his services to create a computer code that could help us get back the control of our computer from Alexander.

While Daniel was explaining the whole intent to them, one of the officials accompanying Mr. Rawat started fidgeting in his chair and a strange look came on his face as if he wanted to say something. As soon as Daniel finished what he was saying, he, Mr. Khosla, started before anyone also could say anything,

"Could you tell us a bit more about that person you are looking for?"

Daniel motioned at Neville to tell him about Param.

"The person we are looking for is Param. He had told me that He had graduated from some big institute, and, if I remember the name correctly, it was Indian Institute of Technology (IIT) in Delhi. We had met at an online convention of White-Hat Hackers and at that time, he was pursuing his Masters Degree at the same institute. We never met in person but used to meet online almost every other day. He is about six-feet tall, bearded, with slightly longish hair . . . ."

"And he is slightly eccentric with a habit of over-elaborating a point of discussion to prove his point . . . ."

"Yes, yes . . ." responded Neville, with visible excitement.

"And had lost his parents in a road accident when he was in the last year of school, and, since his relatives had thrown him out of his ancestral house, he has virtually no one in his family . . . ."

"You know him quite well else you would not know all this. Don't you?"

"Can you tell us where is he right now? We would like to meet him at the earliest," intervened Daniel.

"Yes. As a matter of fact, we can meet him today itself if you do not have any other plans," said Mr. Khosla.

"Today! That is absolutely fantastic," responded Daniel.

At this point, Mr. Rawat, who was looking at Mr. Khosla quite quizzically, asked Mr. Khosla, "How do you this Param?"

To that, Mr. Khosla gave a simple smile and said, "Even you know him sir. In fact, you have met him on several occasions in the last year-and-a-half."

"I know him!" said, Mr. Rawat in a tone of sheer disbelief.

"Yes sir, you know him. The only difference is that he (pointing at Neville) knows him as Param and you know him as Veer i.e. By his middle name. His full name is Param Veer Singh, the Senior Research Analyst at the Cyber Division in our organization whom I had hired about a year-and-a-half ago after he had helped us thwart a cyber attack by our two menacing neighbors."

"Oh! So they are looking for Veer. Yes, I know him and am really proud of his exploits in the short time he has spent with us. But, what is this thing about his research in Sanskrit?" asked Mr. Rawat.

"Sir, if you remember, when we hired him, he had told us about his research for his Ph.D. and had put a condition before us that he would work for straight twenty days in a month and would, then, leave for 10 days at a stretch, and while we had accepted that condition, you were wondering about the topic of his research and he had said that he would inform us once everything was in order," said Mr. Khosla.

"Yes, I remember that."

"Well. That is the topic of his research, "Use of Sanskrit as the root language of a computer to increase its speed, power and efficiency" and he has been working quite hard at it. From what I know, he has a team of about twenty programmers, all of them his friends, who have been working on that project by putting together all their incomes, their grant money, and independent funding. I think they have their lab in Rohini (an area in North Delhi). However, luckily, we would not have to go that far. Today, he is working in office. So, from here, Vasant Vihar, to our office is the only distance we have to cover. So, if you are ready, we can meet him in less than 30 minutes," explained Mr. Khosla.

And, true to his words, we reached the RAW headquarters in less than 30 minutes. But, we did not get out immediately. Mr. Khosla and Mr. Rawat got out of their car and went inside to get all Security-Cams, Microphones and Computers disconnected as per the information given by us that those were Alexander's eyes and ears. He had an eye in the sky as well but there was hardly anything we could do about it. Our main intention was to prevent him from listening to our conversations. And, in keeping with that, they got everyone to switch off their phones and kept all of them in a locker. Once all that was taken care of, we got out of our car and went inside. We were taken to a conference room in one of the Sub-Basement levels. Mr. Khosla and Mr. Rawat joined us in the room in another five minutes and accompanying them was Mr. Param Veer Singh.

Neville immediately got up and went to him to greet him. Mr. Singh was pleasantly surprised at seeing Neville. After all, they were meeting after a long gap of two-and-a-half years, and more importantly, they were seeing each other in person for the first time in their friendship of almost five years.

After a round of introductions, Mr. Khosla spoke to Mr. Singh thus:

"Veer, I always used to wonder if there was anything worthwhile in your research. But, today, I have the proof right in front of my eyes. These people have come here looking for your support in the biggest Cyber project of all time. For almost a month or so, you and your team here at RAW have been working hard trying to bolster our security against this Cyber-terrorist called Alexander . . . ."

"Yes, and we have failed miserably. After all, he has a super computer at his disposal, which we do not", said Param cutting him short.

"And that is where we can help you", intervened Daniel, "We can provide you with a supercomputer. We already have one and we have been working hard to prepare it for a showdown against Alexander. We have almost completed the programming for the same but we believe it is not enough. Neville here told us about your research into Sanskrit and its possible use in computer programming. We are extremely interested in that idea and wish to use that to our advantage. However, the problem is that we do not know anything about Sanskrit and since we do not know the language, we cannot use it in our machine. So, we would like you to be the part of our team and help us fulfill our mission."

"I understand the critical nature of your project and would love to be a part of the project if my government allows me to do so," said Param.

Then, it was my time to intervene and I said, "But the big question that we are facing is how would we be able to transform everything in the machine with only one person working on it with the knowledge of the new language?"

"Do not worry about that. I have a team of twenty computer experts, some of the best minds in the country in this field, who have been working alongside me for the last few years and know everything I know about my idea and are as competent with the language as I am. If you would allow me, I would like to bring them on board for the mission. It is a fact that I alone would not be able to manage everything, I need a team as your existing team would not be able to help me at all. I have the team that knows our hardware, our software and all the basic principles behind our research," replied Param.

Everybody looked at Daniel and he did not take even a moment to accept his proposal. Thus, it was decided that Param and his team would fly over to Charleston to join our existing team. However, had all of us left together, Alexander would have noticed the movement. Therefore, Daniel suggested:

"We would need to ensure that we escape Alexander's notice. All of us would have to take different routes. Use various entry points like New York, Miami, Boston, Chicago, Los Angeles and Dallas to reach the states, and from there, take some road route and rail route to reach Charleston, West Virginia. Once there, we need to ensure we do not stay in same hotels. We need to decide on who would stay in which hotel. Once everyone is in Charleston, we would make arrangements for their transfer to our secure site one by one. So, right now, we need to make a list of who all are joining us, what route would each one by following, what hotels would each one be staying at and by when would they reach there. Once we have decided all that, we would need to put that into action immediately. We need to ensure that we have that list ready in the next three days so that we have it with us when we return. And, once we have returned, we need to ensure that everyone else reaches the project site within three days after that. Tomorrow, we would leave for Agra and Jaipur for a three day trip as we need to make Alexander believe that we are indeed on a vacation. The fact that we found you so easily has allowed us to fool Alexander a bit more. Another thing that I would like to request is to meet those other twenty people who would be joining us. Would it be possible to meet them today?"

To this, Param replied, "We can. We definitely can. All of us were to gather in our lab tonight to discuss something important. So, if you wish, we can leave for the lab in another couple of hours and meet them there."

We had lunch at the RAW headquarters and after relaxing for a couple of hours, we left for Param's lab in two separate cars. One had Daniel along with Mr. Khosla and Mr. Rawat and the second had I, Neville and Param. We reached his lab at Rohini in about an hour. A couple of his friends were already there. They were surprised at seeing the rest of us. Param told them that he would explain everything once all the team members were present. Then, he took us to a conference room. Shortly afterwards, say in about half-an-hour, every team member of Param's team was present in the room with us.

Once everyone was seated, Param introduced us to his team and explained the reason of our visit. He also told them that he had proposed that his whole team should accompany him and the same had been accepted. He, then, asked all of them if they would like to work on the project with him. Everyone looked at each other and in a few moments, one by one, everyone had expressed their acceptance of the offer. So, we had a new team for ourselves.

*   *   *

As planned, we went out to visit the Taj Mahal at Agra and the Pink City, Jaipur, for about two-and-a-half days. By the time we returned, Mr. Khosla, Mr. Rawat and Param had already prepared the list of the team members along with details of the routes everyone was taking; the names, addresses and contact details of the hotels where everyone was to stay; and the approximate time when they could be picked from that location.

We went through the list and found that they had done an excellent job. Almost everyone was taking a different route like via Dubai, Abu Dhabi, London, Frankfurt, Paris, Amsterdam, Zurich, Brussels, Doha, Hong Kong, Istanbul, etc. with a couple of them flying straight from New Delhi to the States on Air India and United, one of them being Param. They, then, planned on taking a further connection to a nearby city and then, either take a train to Charleston or drive down in a rental. As for their Visas, before leaving for Agra, Daniel had already had a word with the Ambassador, and, all the Visas were taken care of in less than two days.

Once we had scanned the list around three times to ensure there were no loose ends, and all of us were ready to leave, Param said, "There is something that I would like to discuss. I believe we should have one more person on our team."

"One more person! Who? Why?" asked Daniel.

"For the last six years, I have been in constant touch with a cyber expert. We have become good friends over time and have been studying each other's work for these last six years. Looking at his work and knowing of his feats, I believe he is one of the best in the trade. Therefore, I believe we should have him in our ranks. The best thing that he will bring to our program is trickery. He is definitely the best in the league when it comes to tricking the system."

"But who is he?" asked Daniel again.

"Prometheus"

"Prometheus?"

"Well . . . . that is not his real name. That is what he goes by with, in the cyber world," said Param.

"Do You mean Prometheus-the Fire God?" I asked.

"Yes . . . . Yes . . . . Do you know him?"

"Every hacker with any bit of talent knows Prometheus and about his exploits. I say he would be a good addition to the team if we are able to find him."

"I know where he lives," said Param.

"Oh! And I thought no one knew where he lived."

"Well . . . . we are good friends. He gave me his physical address last year. He lives in Chicago. We can definitely ask for his help. In fact, I believe we SHOULD ask for his help."

It was decided that I and Neville would accompany Param to go and ask Prometheus to help us out once Param reached USA. We were to go to Chicago, where he lived, by train and bring him to Charleston.

PROMETHEUS

Param arrived at DC by a United flight arriving early morning at Dulles International. He went to the Washington Union Train Station straight from the airport and bought a ticket on the 11 AM train to Chicago. We boarded the same train, 51 Cardinal, from Charleston at around 2000 hours. The train reached Chicago at around 1000 hours next morning. Once we got down at the Chicago Union Station, Param took a cab to reach Oak Park Train Station, which was a short distance from the address that Prometheus had given to Param. The two of us took a separate cab to reach that place. Once we reached there, we found him waiting for us about a hundred meters short of the station. From there, he joined us in our cab and we went to the address at Forest Avenue that Prometheus had given to him.

When we arrived at the house, I could not help but be impressed by the house. It was a nice suburban style house with a well-maintained garden that ran around the house all the way from the front to the sides and the back. There was a driveway from the road to the house on the right of the garden. From the driveway, a stone path led to the front porch. We went up there and Param rang the doorbell. I must say it was a beautiful house, but not because of any grandiose but for its simple charm that each and every inch exuded. The door was opened by an elderly woman who, as we later came to know, was Prometheus' mom and had been living with Chris because of her bad health. When we told her that we wanted to meet with Chris Forlin (Prometheus' real name), she inquired about the reason we wanted to meet him and about who we were. We introduced ourselves as his friends and told her that Param had come all the way from India to meet him. She invited us in and asked us to wait in the living room while she called Chris from the basement. I am quite sure that Chris must have been thrilled to hear about Param as it did not take him more than a couple of minutes to join us in the living room and his heavy breathing suggested that he must have climbed the stairs quite quickly.

Chris wasn't a young man like us. He was at least Forty if not more. It was surprising for me to see such nice friendship between two men belonging to two different age groups and who were quite different from each other in almost every sense. Param was only twenty-six compared to Chris' Forty. Chris was an American while Param was an Indian living half-a-world away. Param had an athletic built and was almost as tall as I am whereas Chris was chubby and not tall by any standards.

Param and Chris met quite warmly. Param introduced us to Chris and explained the purpose of our visit. After hearing all the details, Chris said,

"Why should I help you guys? Your government has always tried to block hackers like us. I have always tried to uphold the best interests of our country and our countrymen but the government has never appreciated my efforts. Today, you have come to me because some lunatic is beating you on your own turf and at your own game. However, once it will all be over with, I would again be forgotten and would again be put under restrictions. So, again, why should I help your government?"

To that I replied, "From what I know of Prometheus, he doesn't care about his personal gains and profits but of the gains and profits he can make for the cyber world. Keeping that in mind, I believe you would help us in any way that you can. Till sometime back, the freedom on the net was somehow restricted and the governments used to watch over each and everything, and used to put limits on our attempts and endeavors. Today, that role has been snatched from the hands of the government and is now in the hands of one individual and he controls and restricts everything. He has the power to cripple the whole Internet if he wanted to, like he did with the stock markets around the world and the Banking Networks. I seriously believe that you are not the kind of person who would let such a thing happen."

"How can you have any belief about what I can or cannot do? You don't know me"

"I do know you. In fact, I knew about your identity and address even before Param gave us that info. I just kept that fact to myself."

"And . . . . how did you get all that information?"

"Well . . . . we had a face-off about three years ago. That's how"

"Face-off! . . . . I have had several opponents over the last few years but nobody could beat me or come to know of my identity . . . . unless . . . . unless you are . . . ."

"YES. I am THE Robin"

"Oh . . . my . . . . God . . . . I never thought we would come face to face ever," said Chris while vigorously shaking my hand.

Then, it was time for Param to exclaim, "I seriously cannot believe that I will be working on a project alongside ROBIN. I mean . . . . for the last four years or so, every hacker in the world has been working wholeheartedly towards achieving one goal—to beat the defense mechanism created by Robin. And, I have the opportunity to work with him and I had no idea about it till now."

Neville added, "Think about me. I have been working with him for the last two-and-a-half years and even I had no idea about it. And, I am pretty sure no one in the complete project team had any idea about it else he would have been put on a pedestal by now not that he isn't already. I always thought that Robin is your real name and the mighty ROBIN of the digital world was using a pseudo."

"Well . . . . only Howard and his bosses knew about it," I said.

"But, I don't understand one thing. If YOU are already a part of the team, why do you need me?" asked Chris.

"First, I am not the kind of person who is too proud to take anyone's help if it is required. Second, it is too big a project to take any chances and we can use all the good brains we can find. Third, you were the only one to pose a serious threat to my defense mechanism. You were the only one to come up with such a serious attack that got me real nervous. And, the only one about whom I did not report to the authorities as I found out that your intentions weren't bad like others," I replied.

"Good . . . . good . . . . now you have got my nerves tingling. I am ready to work with you. But, one thing is bothering me for the last three years. After our "face-off", I tried to find out about your identity out of curiosity. However, the more I looked, the stranger it got for me. For a person who is almost a legend among his contemporaries in the digital world, you have no digital footprint whatsoever. The only information I could find out was about your college where you were enrolled. But, when I checked out your details, I found out that they were all bogus. You somehow managed to get the college authorities to accept those details as authentic but, they were definitely fake. You used the name John Webbon, but, I could not find any details for any John Webbon in any database on the planet. It is as if you do not exist. Leave alone anything else, I couldn't even find out your real name. So, can you tell me your real name?" asked Chris.

"It may sound clichéd but didn't Shakespeare say 'What's in a name?' . . . . I do not think telling anyone about my real name would make any difference to who I am. And, I kind of like the name 'Robin'," I replied.

ALEXANDER—
HE CAME, HE SAW,
HE CONQUERED

At this point, I believe it would be good to tell all of you about what had Alexander been doing for those thirty days that we had spent trying to devise ways and means to fight him.

Once Alexander had taken over the control of CYBERION-1, his first action was to take control of all Military Installations around the world along with the complete weapons arsenal in the world that was computer controlled. That meant that he had all the major weapons under his control like Missiles of all kinds, Air planes, Ships, Carriers, Destroyers, Submarines, Radar Installations, Satellites, etc. with only hand held weapons out of his reach. However, the threat of using Nuclear Weapons and other WMDs (Weapons of Mass Destruction), both Chemical and Biological in nature, was enough to prevent anyone from trying to use any force against him or from attempting to take over any military installations back. Moreover, no one knew where to attack as no one had been able to locate Alexander. He had not made any appearance in person and had contacted the world only through his recorded video messages. The only thing known about him was his photograph that used to appear in his video messages. Even though there could not be any threat to him due to his weapons' stockpile, he did not take any chances. Once he had taken control of all computer-controlled weapons that did not require any human intervention, he went ahead and destroyed all arms and ammunition depots in the world. With that he had further limited the strength of the armies of the world and that meant that he had become even more powerful than before.

Once he had all the military power in the world in his hands, he moved on to other things. He took control of the Banking network around the world. He locked out all bank vaults around the world that had electronic controls. He did not stop any banking operations but released a message to all bank managements around the world stating that he would let the operations continue as long as they worked as per his regulations. He emptied all the accounts in the world that fell in the following categories:

1. Accounts held by Individuals suspected of involvement in Narcotics trade controlled by Drug Cartels

As per official estimates, the worldwide drug trade was worth as much as $400 Billion. Several unofficial estimates suggested that as much as $1.6 Trillion was locked up in bank accounts of those involved in this illegal and immoral trade to convert such illegal money into clean money. It was a different thing that the actual money controlled by such drug cartels was a much higher number as most of it was held in form of cash or precious metals or precious stones. Nobody could understand that move by Alexander. On one hand, he was attempting at creating anarchy by disrupting normal political and economic order of the world, and, on the other hand, he was trying to destroy the crime syndicates working around the world.

2. Accounts held by owners and promoters, known and disguised, of Casinos—both Real and Online Casinos

The annual business generated by Casinos around the world, including online operations, was as high as $200 Billion, and some pretty clear estimates suggested that the promoters and owners held as much as $1.5 Trillion in clean money held in Bank Accounts. Alexander swiped all that off from those accounts.

3. Other accounts held by people suspected of any kind of activity controlled by any Crime Syndicate

Taking into account other kinds of Criminal Activities controlled and managed by Crime Syndicates, like Hawala, Betting, Illegal Arms Trade, etc., Alexander cleaned up another $800 Billion from several Bank Accounts.

4. Accounts held by promoters, owners and major share-holders of Private Companies engaged in Weapons' manufacturing, as well as the corporate accounts of those companies

We were able to find out that he cleaned out $2.5 Trillion from such accounts. In effect, he rendered all such companies with no means to continue any operations. Once he had taken out all the money from their accounts, he launched missiles to destroy all the manufacturing facilities of those companies. That meant that there could not be any more weapons built by the private sector for anyone. The biggest impact was on the supply of hand held weapons and their ammunition. And, since those were the only ones usable against him, it meant that sooner or later, there would not be any weapons in the world outside his control.

Thus, in total, he had cleaned off about $6.4 Trillion from the banks around the world. That was a mind-boggling figure and it was almost hard to believe that someone had the ability to bring the whole banking operations in the world to their knees. But, with world's most advanced and the best computer at his disposal, Alexander managed to do that. The best part was the speed with which all that was done. We assumed that he had already gathered the knowledge about those accounts before-hand and therefore, his only task was to break-in and enter and take the money, which he managed at an incredible speed. His takeover of the Defense systems and the Banking networks was only a day's work for him. When he took over the Banking networks, he issued a stern warning that in case any bank attempted to force open its vaults or to disconnect their networks' outside connections in any way, there would be immediate strikes on that bank to destroy it. And, when a couple of banks did not pay heed to his warning and tried to open their vaults, he immediately fired a missile on each of them and completely destroyed them. He recorded the action against the banks and relayed it to all the television networks in the world. That was enough for the other banks to forget about going against his orders.

The next day, he broke into the systems of all the Stock Exchanges of the world at one go. Not all of them were operating at that time, but, he did it as soon as the NYSE and NASDAQ opened up. He probably did so to make use of the biggest stock exchanges in the world to put his work into effect. By that time, the markets in Asia had closed down, but, Europe was still open. So, he attacked all the Stock Exchanges in the Western Hemisphere simultaneously. He shut them down indiscriminately and kept shutting down one exchange after another till all of them were left inoperative. He, then, took control of the systems of the other exchanges that weren't open till then, but, since their computer systems were still operating, he had the opportunity to take over their controls as well. After he had taken over all the exchanges, he splashed a video message across all television networks in the world that said:

"I HAVE TAKEN CONTROL OF ALL THE STOCK EXCHANGES IN THE WORLD AND HAVE LEFT THEM INOPERATIVE. FROM NOW ON, THERE WOULD BE NO MORE TRADING IN STOCKS AND COMMODITIES OF ANY KIND. ANY ATTEMPT TO WREST THE CONTROL BACK OR AT FINDING AN ALTERNATIVE SOLUTION WOULD FORCE ME TO TAKE APPROPRIATE ACTION AGAINST THE PEOPLE INVOLVED. STOCK TRADING IS AN IMMORAL WAY ADOPTED BY BUSINESSES WORLDWIDE TO EARN MONEY. I WOULD SOON FORMULATE NEW POLICIES REGARDING SELLING SHARES IN A COMPANY TO RAISE CAPITAL, AND, BUYING AND SELLING OF SHARES IN ALL

THE EXCHANGES WOULD BE AS PER THOSE POLICIES."

It took him three days to come up with new guidelines regarding stock trading. As per the new guidelines, he mandated that the trading of shares would be possible with a minimum holding period of 365 days. He also devised a formula for calculation of the price of a share in a company. As per his formula, he did away with any premium on a share's value. He fixed the value of a share in a company during the initial offering as ten units of the currency in which the capital is to be raised. That meant that every share debuting on the bourses was to open at a standard rate of 10 per share. Then, as per his policy, the price of a share was to be decided by the exchange on a quarterly basis depending on the financial reports provided by the company for that quarter. The shares were to be bought or sold only at that fixed price and not at any other price. He released those mandates with the message that those guidelines were meant to prevent profiteering by a few individuals and corporations at the cost of the masses. He also made it mandatory for the companies offering their shares for sale in the open market to dilute at least fifty percent of the total number of shares in the company.

Along with his control of the stock markets, he had taken control of the Commodity trading markets as well and he released new policies for them as well. As per the new policies, he allowed trading for all commodities only for actual physical sales and not for virtual trades involving no actual transfer of any goods. The trading was divided into two categories, International Trade and Domestic trade. For International trades, the trading was limited to the amount of commodity that was surplus from the requirement of that commodity in the region from where it originated. For example, if there was a requirement of 10000 Tonnes of Sugarcane in Brazil's local markets, and, the production was 15000 Tonnes, there was a surplus of 5000 Tonnes or 33.33% of the total production of Sugarcane in Brazil. According to that calculation, his policies stated that every trader was to be allowed to sell only 33.33% of the total stock of Sugarcane held by him to any trader outside Brazil. Also, the cost per unit of the commodity was to be fixed by the exchange as per the financial details provided by the government regarding the production cost of that commodity. Also, the per unit cost of the commodity was to fixed by the exchange as per the financial details provided by the government regarding the production cost of that commodity. As for Domestic Trades, the traders were divided into various groups; Producers, Distributors, Wholesalers, Retailers, and Exporters. The trading was to be done only between traders belonging to different groups as per the price fixed by the exchange for the same. Every successive trader was allowed to increase the price by a maximum of 10 percent to cover their costs and profits.

Alexander had taken control of the Forex Trading platforms as well, and, instead of coming out with any policies for their operations and regulation, he simply closed them down. As per his video message to that effect, leave alone any foreign exchange of currency, there should not be any separate currency, and, there should be only a single currency operating in the world, and, that is what he was aiming at.

His third major action was ordering the closure of all such establishments that he perceived to be aiding in the rise of criminal activities. Such establishments included Casinos, Bars and pubs of all kinds, Shops selling Alcohol, Shops selling Arms and Ammunition, Shops selling Pornography, Establishments for legalized Prostitution, and etc. He also ordered closure of businesses such as production of Alcohol, Tobacco products, and etc. He gave a time limit of two days to comply with the orders failing which he threatened immediate strikes on the cities where such establishments existed. As a warning, he fired a couple of missiles at an alcohol production facility in United States and completely destroyed it.

Alexander had tried to force his policies on all the governments but the governments decided to try and get back the control by force. At that, Alexander launched nuclear missiles at all major cities with seats of governance like Washington DC, London, Delhi, Beijing, Paris, Tokyo, Moscow, and several other cities, and, destroyed all those cities along with all the government offices and heads of governments. Then, where there were standalone government installations in a city, he fired smaller ballistic missiles to destroy those buildings. After that, he had complete control of all major countries of the world like the US, Russia, India, China, UK, France, Germany, Japan, Italy, etc. and once he had taken them over, the smaller countries simply surrendered without a fight.

I wasn't quite sure at that time whether what he was doing was good or bad, but, I never accepted it at right.

PARAM'S VIEWS

Once Chris had agreed to leave with us, we did not waste away any time and decided to take the first train back to Charleston. We took two separate cabs to reach the Chicago Union Square station to catch the evening train to Charleston. Both the cabs reached the station almost at the same time. We bought tickets one after another so we were seated together on the train. Once the train had left the station and we had adjusted our luggage in the overhead compartments, we decided to go to the lounge. We settled down in the lounge facing each other with a table in between.

"So Param, how exactly do you think Sanskrit would help us in our endeavor? You say that it is the best language for the core programming of the computers but I don't understand how can a language affect the performance of a machine? What is the special thing in this language that is not in the other languages?" asked Chris.

Before Param could answer that, I said, "I thought you would know all about it. Neville here knows Param for a lot lesser period than you do but he seems to know a lot about Param's research. On the other hand, your questions seem to convey that you do not know anything about it."

"I do remember that Param had mentioned it about four years ago but that was just once and I do not remember him mentioning it again," replied Chris.

"Yes. I did not mention it again because you had mocked at me when I mentioned it to you for the first time," said Param.

"I am sorry if I did that because I seriously do not remember what had transpired between us at that time. But, now I know that your research is definitely some serious stuff. So, please enlighten me," said Chris with a funny tone, which I believe he did to lighten the mood.

At this, Param smiled a bit, pushed himself a bit towards the back of the seat to relax himself and started to explain his views about Sanskrit:

"Sanskrit isn't simply a language that has come into vogue merely by simple usage, collection of words to create a vocabulary, mix and match of words influenced by migration, mixing of cultures, biological changes in speech mechanism or any other human factor. Sanskrit was a language based on the 'Devanagri' script. 'Devanagri' loosely translates into "The Language of Gods". The basic idea behind Sanskrit is to focus on the energy flowing in the universe and channelize that energy into the human body through speech. By energy here, I am referring to the concept of 'Shakti' as understood in the Ancient Indian Scriptures. It meant the power that created everything living and non-living, that maintains and influences the life and energy of everything material and immaterial, and the one that can reshape the path taken by the life of every being. Various independent researches by several intellectuals and by several institutes focusing on Sanskrit studies have shown that the various elements forming this language focus on various energy cores of the human body, i.e. points that are the gateways of energy flow in the human body and regulate the various mechanisms that are responsible for the functioning of the brain, other body parts, and the innate power of every human being. The various components of this language stimulate all the nerve points of the human body individually as well as in various combinations. And, these combinations are not arbitrary. The language has been constructed in such a manner that it creates only logical combinations and each of those combinations can be further combined into still powerful modes of energy influencing. These higher combinations, called Mantras, when chanted again and again in a proper manner can realign the energy pattern of a person's body in a positive manner. It is a well-known principle of Ancient Indian Philosophy that each and every major celestial body exerts an influence on our lives, our environment and our whole existence. The energy liberated and ingested by these bodies creates a field of influence that extends far into the universe, far enough for them to influence Earth, every being on Earth and everything on Earth. Everyone realizes the influence of the Sun on our planet and on our lives. However, that is merely because of its size and the amount of power liberated by the Sun. However, Sun's energy affects only one domain of 'Shakti' that influences our lives. There are several other domains and those domains are affected by the field of influence of other celestial bodies like the planets around our planet, the constellations and other stars surrounding us. All those various kinds of energies are flowing all around us. By chanting the

Mantras, one can channelize those energies in a way that could influence the particular domain related to that particular kind of energy and, thus, reshape the pattern of their future life. A simple example of the effect of those Mantras can be seen in the effect on health by their usage. Their continuous usage raises energy levels in the body thereby increasing the body's resistance against illnesses; the relaxation of mind that in turn reduces the stress on the mind allowing for clearer and better thought process; activation of various energy centers of the body that help in managing things like Blood Pressure, Oxygen levels, concentration, and etc. And all these have been proven by proper studies in this field. Now, what do you think those mantras are? They are codes created using Sanskrit as the medium and they work with the most complex computer ever known and the biggest one that is possible to exist, the UNIVERSE. If this language can work there, it can work anywhere. Contrary to popular belief, Sanskrit is not a hard language to learn. In fact, due to its systematic construction and adherence to clear sounds, it is perhaps a language that can be learnt much more easily than any other language that has ever existed in this world. Once a person has learnt the Sanskrit Alphabet, he moves on to learn the finer nuances of the Sanskrit grammar, the most important of them being the 'VIBHAKTI'. It is the tense ending and is the feature that gives Sanskrit its scientific precision."

After a momentary pause, he continued, "Now, when we talk about Sanskrit and its usage in Computers, there are three features of the language that are of most use to us. One, the order of words in a sentence has no bearing on the meaning of the sentence. The structural formation of the language is such that while composing a meaningful sentence, it does not matter what is the position of any word in the sentence and any rearrangement would not alter the meaning of the sentence. This is mainly because of the fact that there are no proper nouns in Sanskrit. All words are derived from the characteristic of an object or a being due to which every word has a meaning built into the root of the word and there isn't any word in the language that is meaningless and has been constructed arbitrarily to signify an object. The second is the Derivative potential of the language. There are words that can be generated in this language for each and every object and being ever known and each and every object and being that will ever be known to mankind. Even though the number of nounal and verbal roots is limited, those limited roots can be used with several prefixes, suffixes and inflections to create an unlimited number of words. The third is the possibility of expansion and contraction that can be achieved with this language. The same meaning can be conveyed in multiple ways, with a limited number of words and with a large number of words as well. An example to this effect can be found in 'Kadambari', a beautiful novel written by Banabhatta, wherein there is a single word that runs for thirteen printed lines and there is a single sentence that runs beyond twenty printed pages."

*   *   *

After Param had explained everything to us, all of us were lost in our thoughts trying to grasp more of what he had said and how could it be implemented.

"Interesting . . . . Quite interesting . . . ," said Param.

I turned my head to look at him and found him looking quite intently at the blue file that I had kept on the table quite absentmindedly. He suddenly glanced up and caught me staring at him. I believe he could read my face and saw the questions floating all over as he explained his remark,

"This name . . . . You say it is **Alexander Ajanma** (pronounced Ahanma) but this last name, when read not as a Hispanic name but as a name in normal English is quite different. You assumed it to be Hispanic pronouncing 'J' as 'H' but if you just read 'J' as it is, like in JUST or JOHN, the pronunciation would have an Indian link."

"How?" I asked him.

"**AJANMA** [(**A** (as in **A**MONG)—JA (as in **J**OHN)—N (as in BEG**UN**)—MA (as in PU**MA**)]."

"What is **AJANMA**?" I asked.

"I guess you have no idea about the Hindu philosophy about God."

"To be honest, you are right. I hardly know anything about India, and even less so about Hindus and their religion," said I with a shrug of my shoulders.

"**AJANMA** means **UNBORN** in its literal sense. However, when we speak in Theosophical terms, it means, **'One who did not take birth'** referring to the ultimate power, the one who did not take birth from anything but from whom everything else took birth like the planets, the stars, the seen, the unseen, everything from sub-atomic particles to the biggest celestial body, or, in short, the whole cosmos was born out of him. So, **AJANMA** is usually a reference to **GOD**, the cause of all causes," explained Param.

"That really is something very interesting. I wish that assessment could help us in some way," I said with a deep sigh.

The fact was that we had no idea about the identity of Alexander despite our best possible efforts to that effect. He was an enigma that had given us sleepless nights and we were still as directionless as a drunken man wandering around in a location unknown to him. I remember that I had spent at least ten minutes thinking over it while staring blankly at the sky through the window.

A TRYST WITH DEATH

About ten minutes after Param had finished explaining his views about Alexander's last name to us, a man walked up to us with his laptop and asked if there was someone named Robin in the group. When I told him that he was referring to me, he kept his laptop on the table and turned the screen towards me. And, the moment I looked at the screen, I realized the reason why was he looking for me. There was a live transmission from Alexander on the screen, with his picture on the screen. Like his previous broadcasts and messages, I understood that even that was only a still picture and only his voice would be heard. As soon as it had my attention, he spoke:

"So . . . . Mr. Robin . . . . You thought you would be able to escape my notice by resorting to those small tricks. Did you forget what you created with CYBERION-1? Did you forget that it could see everywhere and at everyone at all times? I know what you are up to. You are gathering all kinds of computer experts and are assembling a team to try to beat me. First, you went to India to ask Mr. Singh to join you. Hello Mr. Singh. How are you? Are you enjoying this little adventure of yours? I am sure you are. After all, it is quite a break from your routine at RAW. And, how are you Mr. Forlin, or, should I say PROMETHEUS? He is the second person you are taking with you to your facility near Charleston. Oh! . . . . (Probably reading the change of expression on my face through the webcam) . . . you thought I didn't know about it. I know all about it. About your facility, about MAXIMUS, about your team, about the team that has joined you from India, about everything. I am sure you are surprised that I did not do anything about it till now. Well . . . to be honest, I wanted to give you a chance to stage a fight-back. A fight using weapons isn't my preference as it causes only destruction and nothing else and, also, because you would not stand a chance against me in that respect. Therefore, I was looking at a war of the brains and I believe all of you have a right to a fight. But, since then, I have had second thoughts and after recalculating my risk at giving such a chance, and after my reassessment of the capabilities of MAXIMUS, I have decided not to allow you to go ahead with it. Therefore, after due consideration and with a sad heart for all the collateral damage that would be caused by my next action, I am sorry to say that I have decided to take all of you out of the picture. In moments, I will launch a couple of AMPERIA missiles that would hit your train in a matter of minutes. And, as soon as I will launch them, you would see a counter on this screen with the time left for the missile to strike the train. I am doing this to give you a chance to try and save yourself. You have all the freedom to do whatever you want to do to save yourself and the others on the train. You can make calls or you can make use of any computer or any other gadget. The only thing you cannot do is to try and pry the doors open. So . . . best of luck and . . . . Goodbye."

By that time, everyone around us had gathered near our seats as they could all hear whatever Alexander was telling me. Once his transmission ended, there was a dead silence in the car. I immediately told the guy whose laptop it was that we would need it to try and do something about the missiles. He was still wide-eyed from what he had heard and simply nodded in affirmative. I got down to finding details about the Amperia missiles. At that very moment, a time-counter appeared on the screen to tell us that Alexander had launched the missiles and we just had ten minutes left to do anything about it. It took me a few seconds to pull up the details of the missiles. We found out that they are long-range missiles with pin-point accuracy. In addition to them being guided missiles using their in-built radar, they had heat-seeking ability as well that gave them the ability to track moving objects using their heat signature allowing them quicker adaptation to sudden route alteration by the target. We looked out the window and saw that we were going through an open countryside and there wasn't any other major object or building in sight. Suddenly, something struck Neville. He took the laptop from me and started searching for something online. In a minute, he informed the rest of us that there might be a solution to the crisis. He told us that he had seen a huge building while on the way from Charleston to Chicago. He had just caught a glimpse of it when he got up in the night to take a leak. He had looked up online to find out what it was and had found out that it was a steel plant that was operational and operated round the clock. It was one of the few steel plants in the United States that still worked in the traditional mould. It had been upgraded partially a few years back but, in any case, a steel plant meant a lot of heat. He said that if we could pass through that particular point right at the time when the missiles reached near the train, the heat from the plant could confuse the missiles to treat the plant as a target instead of the train.

At that, I calculated the distance between the train and the plant and found out that at the speed the train was travelling, the eight minutes left on the counter would be too less. Param calculated that we had to try and increase the speed of the train by about sixty miles an hour to make it to the plant in time. I asked Chris to take a couple of guys with him and get everyone in all the cars to move to the front of the train, and, then, to disconnect all the empty cars from the train. This was to solve two issues. One, lesser number of cars meant lesser load for the train to pull enabling it to accelerate it to the required speed quickly. Second, the shorter the length of the train, the shorter would it be as a target for the missiles and it would make it harder for the missiles to distinguish between the steel plant and the train. At that, Chris immediately asked for help from two strong guys who looked like they were some football players. I, then, asked another person to lend his mobile phone to me and from that phone, I called up the office of Mr. Rourke. Fortunately, he was available in his office and the call was immediately transferred to him. I quickly told him about our situation and what we were planning to do. I asked him to get the plant evacuated immediately. He gave me an assurance that he would do his best to ensure an empty plant at the time of the strike.

By that time, we had reached the engine and from the internal communication device, that is present on all modern trains, to contact the driver in case of an emergency, and alerted the driver to the emergency and asked him to give us access to the engine car. He hesitated for a few seconds but when a lot of people spoke to him and requested him to open the access, he relented. Upon entering, we told him to increase the speed by another sixty miles i.e. from eighty miles an hour to one hundred and forty miles per hour. In the meantime, the train crew had helped Chris and the others to gather everyone in the first two cars after which, all of them got together to remove the rest of the cars from the train. By the time everything was done, there were only two minutes left on the counter. Param calculated again and asked the driver to reduce the speed by twenty miles to reach one hundred and twenty miles per hour. Soon, the plant was visible in the distance. When there were just thirty seconds left on the counter, Param recalculated and asked the driver to reduce the speed further to reach One hundred miles an hour. His continuous speed alterations worked and we missed the missiles by a whisker as, in accordance with our expectations, they got confused due to the huge heat signature of the plant and struck the plant instead of the train. The plant was blown to bits. The blast was quite powerful and created a shock-wave that almost derailed the train. All the windows got shattered and the glass flew all over and injured almost everyone on the train. However, getting injured by the flying glass was a much better bargain compared to being blown to bits by the missiles.

* * *

The misadventure that we had lived through had shaken us up quite badly and we were still recuperating from it when we reached the next station. The driver had already informed the station authorities and there were paramedics waiting for all the passengers at the station. Some of the passengers were sent to the nearby hospital but most required only minor First aid that was provided by the Paramedics at the station itself. After a few hours, another train was arranged for everyone to continue the onward journey. We reached Charleston next morning. Once we reached there, we went straight to the Car Rental location that was a front for our transport requirements. We took a car to reach the project site. However, when we reached there, we found out that the site had been completely destroyed. There were no security personnel anywhere; the security wall had been blown away to bits along with every other structure; all the vehicles were destroyed and there were dead bodies strewn all over with almost all of them missing some part of their bodies. What we were looking at seemed to us to be the end of the world.

"What the hell happened here?" asked Chris.

"What do you think happened here? It is quite obvious that Alexander had launched some missiles here as well like he did with us. We escaped, but, it seems they (pointing at some of the dead bodies) did not," I replied to his question.

"So, what do we do now?" asked Param.

"Let's go back to Charleston and check all our options. We need to see what can be done now. I am sure there is something else that we can do about it," I replied.

We stayed there for another hour as we went around the place to check if we could find any survivors. However, it seemed that Alexander had ensured that no one could escape his attack. Therefore, even though we felt bad that we had to leave without doing anything about the dead, we had to leave. We went to the Car rental to return the car. He was surprised that we had returned so quickly as in the usual scenario, the car was returned by someone else visiting the city for some supplies or anything else. When he asked us about it, we told him about the site's destruction and our plan of leaving for DC at the earliest. At that he said,

"I was told to inform any survivors in such an event to go to Mr. Charles Witnick, who lives just outside the city, on the end opposite to the one leading to the site. I was told that he has some information that is of utmost importance to anyone associated with the project in case the site is attacked and is lost."

We immediately asked him to lead us to Mr. Witnick not only because we were curious about what information did he have about the site that was not available to us, but also because we were feeling desperate to find a solution to the crisis.

Mr. Witnick lived at a farm about ten miles outside Charleston. When we reached there, we found him tending to the plants in the greenhouse adjacent to the side lawn. Mr. Witnick was at least Sixty Years old but was quite sturdy and well-built for his age. When we went up to him, the guy from the Car Rental outlet, Garry, pointed to the four of us and simply said one word,

"MAXIMUS"

That was enough for Mr. Witnick to understand the reason why we were there. He came up to us and said,

"Hi. I am Charles Witnick. You can call me Charles. I get it that you are from the MAXIMUS project. And, the fact that you are here tells me that something bad has happened at the project site. Am I right?" asked Charles.

"Yes. You are right. Our project site has been completely destroyed. I believe it was struck by missiles. We couldn't find anyone alive there. There were only dead bodies and bits and pieces of bodies strewn all over and the rest are probably buried under the rubble to be fished out. Garry here told us that you have some important information to provide us," I replied.

"Well . . . . You believe that the project site has been completely destroyed but that is not the truth. It has been razed to the ground but it has not been destroyed completely," said Charles.

"What are you trying to say?" asked Neville.

"We saw everything destroyed. We went around the whole site and there isn't anything that escaped destruction," added Chris.

"Well . . . . I am sure that none of you are fully conversant with the structural strength of your project site and the safeguards that have been built into the building complex."

"What safeguards?" asked Param.

"Well . . . . First of all, have you forgotten about the fact that the complex has multiple levels beneath the ground level? Those levels had been constructed in such a manner that they could survive even a small nuclear blast, especially the lower levels. Now, I am sure that the attack on MAXIMUS wasn't nuclear else it would have caused a lot more destruction. So, you can believe me when I say that MAXIMUS and most of your team are still safe. The impact of the blast would not have reached the lower levels and the rubble would not have had any impact on the structure apart from the fact that it would have blocked the access to the lower levels. The only problem is that we cannot open the access channels without removing the rubble, and, if we try and remove the same, we will have to move some machinery there and it would be noticed by Alexander. Therefore, we cannot go to the project site to access the lower levels, we will have to do it from another point."

"Do you mean dig in from some other location? I believe it would take a lot of time and I am not sure if they would survive for that long. Also, the structure might collapse if we dig in the wrong way," said Neville.

"Are you all from the new team that had joined the MAXIMUS project about a month ago?" asked Charles.

"Yes," I replied.

"Well . . . . That explains it. You guys are not aware of the whole construct. All the equipments and resources to run the site are located at the lowest level. Therefore, there is no way that they could have been affected by the blasts. That means that the people stuck there have about a week before there is any impact on their normal routines. The operations would keep running in the normal manner even without any external supplies for a week. The air control unit has vents that open up about half a mile away so even they should be intact. The power sub-station, cooling plant, and everything else was designed to withstand such attacks."

"So . . . would we be going in through the air vents?" asked Chris.

"Well . . . . The vents are not big enough for anyone to pass through. They are tiny holes built in by boring small holes through a rock face."

"So, how do we get in?" I asked.

"Well . . . the engineers had built a safeguard to tackle such a crisis. There is an opening about five miles away from the project site that gives access to a tunnel that opens into the tunnel that houses the Power Sub-station . . . ."

"Wait . . . . Wait . . . . Wait . . . . Wait . . . . Wait . . . I have been to the Sub-station at least five times, but I have not seen any opening there," I said while interrupting him.

"I am sure you did not. You are not the only one. No one from the staff could see it. It is not supposed to be visible to anyone till the time there is any actual need for it. The northern end of the tunnel has a moveable wall that separates the two tunnels and can be opened only with a mechanical lever that is located in the outer tunnel. Once that lever is activated, the partition gives away and simultaneously, another lever panel appears in the inner tunnel as well. The access to the outer tunnel is controlled by a mechanical lever system in turn. The engineers had kept everything mechanical intentionally so that even if there is a power failure or damage to the computer systems, the tunnel would not be affected and there would not be a problem with the access . . . ."

"So . . . . How do we get to that access point?" I asked.

"We will need to leave for that point early in the morning as we cannot reach that point in any vehicle. We would need to trek for about ten miles through a forest after a drive of about forty miles. Since it is almost evening now, it would be better if we leave at the break of dawn instead of right now as it would not be easy to trek at night through that dense vegetation," said Charles.

With that, we went to his house and spent the night making arrangements for the next day's trek.

THE END
OF TIME

Access Point

The next morning, we got up at four in the morning and by five, we had already left Charles' place. Garry sat with Charles in his truck while the four of us drove off in the other car. We followed his truck and after about thirty-odd miles, we entered a forest area. He took us deep inside that area. After another ten miles inside the forest, we came across a barricade manned by four army men. Charles had a word with them but we could not hear anything as we were at a bit of a distance. I do not know what he said to them but the barricades were removed in a jiffy. We drove for another couple of miles after crossing that check-point before we reached a dead-end. At that point, we got off our vehicles and took out all the necessary gear that we had brought with us as per the instructions given by Charles. All of that stuff was available in his garage. He told us that he had stored all of it as he knew that it might be needed some day. We got ready for the trek and loaded ourselves with all the equipment.

"This is a protected forest area that is blocked from all around. There is a perimeter fence running all around with barricades at three entry points that are manned round the clock by army personnel. The fencing is atop a perimeter wall and is electrified. The wall is to prevent the animals from getting electrocuted by the fencing. So, no one has ever had access to this zone. We did this to prevent anyone from accidentally discovering the access point to the tunnel that leads to MAXIMUS. The access point is about ten mile east from here. However, we did not build any roads to that point intentionally so that it remains as inaccessible as possible. The trek from this point to the access point is quite difficult. That is why we need to be quite careful with where we step. There are several natural pits and crevices that are not easily visible due to the dense vegetation. Then, there are animals, snakes, and spiders that may pose a risk as well. That is why, we need to ensure that we do not take off our knee-length boots and we keep our knives and guns handy and ready at all times. So . . . . If you are ready, let's begin," said Charles.

The rest of us nodded in approval and set-off on the trek till the access point.

The trek wasn't easy as the ground was slippery all throughout. It had probably rained there the previous night due to which there was a lot of mud all around and we were finding it difficult to find a good foothold. Due to that, we were progressing at a much slower pace than what we wanted to set. It took us about five hours to cover those ten miles and reach the point, where Charles stopped and asked us to relax and said,

"This is it. That is where the access point is (pointing to a group of rocks). But, it would be good if we rest for a bit. We have been walking continuously for the last five hours. If we relax for a while, we will have our strength back as we would need it to open the access tunnel."

That part of the forest was slightly uphill and it seemed it did not have as much rain as the part from where we started our trek as the ground was dry partly due to less water and partly due to the heat from the sun that had come exactly overhead by that time. We decided to eat something and lie down to catch a wink or two before getting to work with the access tunnel. After resting for about an hour, we got up and got to work.

We went up to that group of rocks that Charles had pointed out. He told us that the rocks were to be removed to uncover the mechanical panel that was to be used to open the entrance to the tunnel. It took us a lot of time and effort to remove the rocks and move them to a distance. The lid of the mechanical panel became visible only after we had removed three-fourths of the rocks. Once we had removed all the rocks, it became evident that it wasn't a small panel. In fact, what we were looking at was the lid of the panel that was about two meters in diameter. There were two keyholes that were covered by small latches to prevent mud from entering and jamming the keyholes. We removed the latches after cleaning the mud that had accumulated all around. We, then, cleared the rest of the lid of mud. Charles pulled out two big keys from his pocket and asked me and Param to unlock the lid. The keys were quite big, at least eight inches in length if not more, and so, we assumed that the levers of the lock would be big as well and it would be a task to open them. But, quite surprisingly, the locks opened as easily as a normal door-lock.

Once we had opened the locks, Charles asked us to take out the rods that he had asked us to bring. The rods were quite unique in design. They were not circular. They were square-edged. They had a small hook-like projection at one end and quite a stylish flower-like hold on the other end with five petals that were at least an inch thick. Charles asked us to insert the hook-like projections into the key-holes and push the rods down till they hit the bottom. We did as he told us to do. Then, he asked us to rotate the rod till we hear a click. He told us that the click meant that the lid was free from the panel and ready to be removed. The lid was quite heavy so all of us had to pitch in to lift it off the control panel.

The control panel had a number of patterns on it. We were expecting some switches or levers but it had nothing of the sort. Charles told us to take the rods out of the lid and invert them. That way, the flower-like hold was at the bottom and the hook was at the top. He asked us to fit the holds of the two rods into two flowers-like patterns on the control panel and to push them down with force. We tried but it did not go down as much as it should have. Then, suddenly remembering something, Charles apologized and too out another rod that he was carrying in his bag. He took it out of the long cloth that it was wrapped in and handed it to us. It was a thick circular rod but wasn't as heavy as its size suggested. It was probably somewhat hollow from inside. It had two square holes, one at each end, about one quarter of the length from the two ends.

Charles asked us to insert the two rods into the holes in that rod from the ends with the hooks. Looking at the square-edged rods, we couldn't make out that there was any variation in width at any place, but, there indeed was a variation. When we pushed the third rod down after inserting the two rods in the holes, it moved down about one-thirds of the lengths of the two rods and then, stopped. We couldn't take it down any further. That rod certainly gave us the much required leverage. It was still quite hard to push down but when all of us made an effort, it went down. Once it had gone down about an inch and a half, we heard a clicking noise. At that, Charles told us to push the panel in anti-clockwise circular motion. Once it had moved about half a circle, it stopped moving. Charles asked us to push down again. The rods went down another couple of inches. He again asked us to move the panel in an anti-clockwise circular direction. It again moved half a circle before stopping. He asked us to push down again. The rods went in another inch and a half. Then, Charles asked us to move the panel in a clockwise circular motion till it completed four full rounds.

We did as we were told and once the four rounds were complete, we heard a rumbling noise behind us. Charles led us to an open area about fifty yards away and we found that the ground had moved down to create an incline going down into a big tunnel.

Charles said, "When we moved that lever over there, it removed the holds that were stopping the steel walls holding this incline up. Four rounds for four walls. The walls have sunk down in the ground at varying depths to create this incline. Let's go down now. About a hundred yards inside the tunnel, we will find a couple of mechanical carts that we can use to reach the project site."

We went down the incline into the tunnel and as he had said, there were a couple of mechanical carts about a hundred yards inside the tunnel. Those were three-wheeled carts that had to be pedaled to make them move.

"Why do you have mechanical carts placed here? Why couldn't you have something like a battery-driven golf cart or something else of the sort?" asked Chris.

"Well . . . . As you must have noticed, and as I had mentioned earlier, everything in this access route is mechanical. When we thought about constructing it, our main idea was to build such a system that would be operative under all circumstances. By keeping everything mechanical, we have done away with situations where we are crippled or stuck due to non-availability of electricity or shortage of fuel or any error due to a computer glitch, etc. and that meant that whether the emergency was due to a missile attack or a nuclear attack or any natural disaster, this system would withstand everything and would remain operational. I must tell you that it can withstand a magnitude 8 earthquake," replied Charles.

"We?" I asked.

"Well . . . . I was a member of the engineering group that constructed this and your project site. I retired after completing this project," replied Charles.

This was news to us but it also explained how Charles knew so much about the site and the access route.

I and Param were the strongest in the group so we were the ones pedaling the two carts while the others were sitting in the back.

Param said, "These carts are almost like the three-wheeled rickshaws that we have in India that are pedaled in the same manner. Tell me something Charles. How is it that the tunnel is lit for us to see the path? You said just now that there is no fuel or electricity in use here. Are you taking electricity from the project site?"

Charles replied, "Oh, no, no, no. we aren't taking anything from the project site. When you turned the levers to open the incline, a solar panel got uncovered as well. That solar panel is powering these lights here and is also storing some juice in a storage panel that will light these in the night."

we reached the end of the tunnel in a few minutes. We got off about fifty yards before the end. Charles went to a side and opened a metal lid that was covering a lever. He pulled the lever down and a metallic panel opened up about twenty yards towards the end wall. The mechanism to move that panel was almost absolutely the same when compared to the one that opened the access to the tunnel. However, at the access point, the walls had gone down into the ground, but here, there was only one wall that went up inside a cavity in the ceiling. Therefore, there was slight change in the working of the panel. The panel had to be moved only once in the final turn. Then, there were four small clamps located at the edge of the circle at equal distance from each other. We had to turn them down to fit them into four slots on the panel so that they acted as brakes and prevented the panel from turning back.

When the end wall receded into the ceiling, we found that the tunnel had opened into the power sub-station. Once in, we went straight to the core control room. Most of the staff was present there. They were all ecstatic to see us. After a couple of minutes of celebrations and mutual hugs, I asked everyone to be present in the control room after a couple of hours for a meeting to work out the strategy to counter Alexander. I asked them to give the message to others as well. Since we had lost Daniel and other seniors in the nuclear explosion in DC, I was the senior-most at the site, and, hence, was in command. I asked for a meeting after two hours to take some time out to relax and settle in.

At the meeting, the first thing I inquired about was the damage to the site. We were informed that only the ground level bore the damage from the missile strikes. The level just below the ground level also bore some amount of damage but it wasn't exactly critical. About the personnel, we were told that all the security personnel were killed in the attack. A few support staff members were lost as well along with a dozen or so from the administrative staff. Though I shouldn't have felt that way, but I must say that I was relieved to hear that no one from the programming team or from the technical team was lost. That meant that we had a good chance to get back on track and complete what we intended to complete.

We created a few groups that were given the duty of bringing in supplies everyday through the tunnel. Since it was a long trek and then, a long drive to the city and the same way back, we decided on only one round a day when a group would go with the list of all the necessities and would bring back as many of the items on the list as possible. And, all the groups were formed of able-bodied men primarily from the support staff and the administrative staff.

THE FIGHT-BACK

It wasn't easy for us to do what we had to do. Apart from the team from India, none of us at MAXIMUS, with the exception of Neville, had any knowledge of Sanskrit, and, there was no way of learning that language in less than a month. Therefore, as was decided, and, was quite obvious, Param's team had the task of translating all the coding prepared by us in Sanskrit and, then, apply it to the system. His team had brought in their own hardware and software to help with the transition. We worked together and devised an inbuilt mechanism wherein the words in all the sentences in all the files would rearrange themselves every minute in case of an attack. The rearrangement was based on the principle of dividing the sentence into words or group of words in a pre-decided manner so that the rearrangement would have no impact on the meaning of the sentence.

We also went ahead and created a program to disrupt any attempt at a translation of the files by another system. At the same time, we created a worm that was to translate all the files of the target system into Sanskrit, then, rearrange the words, and, finally, to leave a code that was to prevent any re-translation.

We worked hard, we worked fast, and we tried our best to not let the pressure get to us in any manner. The twenty-five days we spent trying to develop the coding for MAXIMUS were extremely grueling for us. And, outside, the world order had changed quite a bit. Thankfully for us, there was sufficient money and resources stocked at the project site to allow us to work undetected. Had we not had those reserves, it would have forced us to seek more supplies from the government, which would have brought us to Alexander's notice as he had taken over the governance of the country. In fact, not only the United States, he had taken control of each and every country of the world.

Thus, while we were busy for those twenty-five days at our project site deep underneath the ground, Alexander was busy taking over the world. By the time we were ready with MAXIMUS, he was already the king of the world. He had removed all borders and divisions. In that short span of twenty-five days, the way the world had lived for three millennia had changed. There were no political boundaries anywhere. I had never thought that such a day was even remotely possible where there were no Americans, no British, no French, no Indians, no Chinese, and etc., and everyone was just a human being, a resident of Earth, a citizen of Earth, and not a resident or citizen of any country. But, Alexander managed that. It is different matter altogether that he destroyed more than ninety percent of the world's armies in the process and killed about five hundred million people in total. He destroyed all terrorist camps he could find anywhere on the planet be it of Al Qaeda, Lashkar-E-Taiba, Taliban, Harkat-ul-Mujahideen, Hezbollah, Jaish-E-Mohammed, Hamas, and etc. He also launched air strikes using pilotless drones on any private militia present anywhere on the planet belonging to any weapons' dealer, or any drug cartel or any self proclaimed leader.

Along with the physical world, he was also the leader of the digital world. He had brought together all the Super-computers of the world along with all the individual personal computers and servers present anywhere in the world to create a super network spread across the planet.

Once he had taken over the world, he had decided to rebuild it according to his wishes. He had set-up a planning division, reconstruction division, maintenance division, and a world army. He had sent out messages to select people around the globe to join all those units. He did not make any job offers, he did not ask anyone whether they wanted to join the designated division or not, and did not take their opinions. He simply ordered them to join a specific unit at a specific remuneration. And, whether they wanted or not, everyone joined. One reason was that everyone was scared to defy Alexander's orders, and, second was that the remuneration was excellent. Even though I did not like the way he had gone ahead to fulfill his intentions, I did find some good things in all that. One thing that I truly liked was the fact that all those organizations were truly global organizations. Each and every division had experts belonging to every corner of the world that had brought everyone on the same pedestal. There was no discrimination of any kind in the selection of those personnel.

Once those divisions were in place, he laid out certain ground-rules before them and asked them to work out proposals for him to dwell on, and, once accepted, they were to implement those plans. While asking them to come up with plans, he asked them to concentrate on the benefit of the society rather than profits. While his divisions were concentrating on coming up with some plans, he had his own plans to put in place. He did away with all those businesses that he thought were unsuitable to the growth of humanity. He stopped all kinds of mining activities in the world and got a team of experts on finding alternatives to various metals and minerals obtained by mining. He got another group to go full steam ahead on setting up recycling plants all over the world. He stopped the production of vehicles designated for personal usage and created another team of experts to focus on mass-transit systems all over the world. He created another team to work on setting up solar power plants and wind farms all over the world. He took over the control of all kinds of businesses all over the world to centralize all of them and to eliminate profiteering. It was as if he was trying to make this world a better place but on his terms, and his terms only.

Another major change that he had put in motion was in the field of Robotics. He had designated a large team of scientists and technical experts to work at improving the standards of Robot production. He gave them designs, schematics and layouts for improvement of machinery in the existing production facilities as well as for improvement in the standard of Robots produced by those facilities. He allocated a huge sum of money for that project.

In short, he was bringing in something new almost every day. In some sense, I personally thought that some of his steps were absolutely brilliant. However, the worst part about his plans was the fact that he was absolutely brutal when it came to imposing his will against any hard opposition. For instance, a group of protestors had led a huge procession to Berlin City Center demonstrating against the removal of political boundaries and forcing them to work with people from the so-called 'Third World' countries and keeping them on the same pedestal. He splashed a message on all television screens and advertisement screens present in the area asking everyone to disperse and go back home. But, when no one paid any heed to his warnings, he had a fighter drone drop a 'Class A' bomb on the crowd. The attack killed more than Six Thousand people on the spot and maimed another thirteen thousand from the crowd that had more than a hundred thousand protestors. There were similar protests all over the world, some political, some religious, and some against subjugation. He took a similar approach everywhere. In all those air strikes and land-to-land missile strikes, he killed another twenty million in addition to those he had killed otherwise. Thus, even though his intentions seemed good to a few like me, his methods were totally unacceptable for anyone. Nobody wanted him around.

There was another thing that bothered people a lot. He always maintained contact with the world through his messages that he used to broadcast on the internet and on satellite channels. Everybody had seen his picture in the messages broadcast by him but no one had ever met him in person. No one knew where he lived or where he operated from or who else worked with him. In fact, no one knew anything about him. His only identity was his picture and his voice.

Getting back to our preparations, the program we were working on had a "Relay Mechanism" as well. We were not trying out a simple linear programming standard. We were working on creating a code that linked, in some form or another, to some other part of the whole file system we were creating. This 'connectivity' allowed us to create that "Relay Mechanism". The codes we were writing were 'overlapping codes', which, in simple language, refers to 'a code within a code'. Our main codes were actually sub-codes hidden underneath primary codes. In case of any attack by any other system or on any other system, the primary code was to be the first line of attack and while that engaged with the other system, the sub-code hidden within, which was actually our main weapon, was to launch a counter-attack through a different channel. It was to convert the language of all the files of the other system one by one to make all of them unreadable to that system but readable to our system. In case the primary code appeared to be losing to its adversary, the sub-code was to cut itself from that location and move to a different location. That was to result in that other location getting two sub-codes within a primary code and that was to trigger the creation of two additional files with a replica of those sub-codes but with their words rearranged and realigned to create a different form of those sub-codes that, then, were to act as two different primary codes on their own. Thus, every file destroyed was to result in two new files. Then, there were certain important sub-codes that were so inter-related that once one sub-code entered another file with its own sub-code, the two of them were to amalgamate into a new code altogether and the new code was to replicate itself into as many files as it could rearrange the words of its coding into. That meant that one single file's destruction was to result in as many as twenty new files.

Once our program was ready, we decided that it would be better to launch an attack in the blitzkrieg mode as we did not wish to give Alexander any chance to acquaint and prepare himself against MAXIMUS. We decided to first take control of all satellites and as many bigger computers as possible. That was to allow us as much exposure and attack points against Alexander as possible. Alexander had taken over each and every computer in the world to create a digital brain with each computer working like a "Synapse" works in a human brain and the whole system gave an exponential increase in speed and efficiency to CYBERION-1. By taking over the satellites and some of the smarter computers, we were to reduce his resources considerably and increase ours at the same time. And, once inside the networks, we were hoping to gradually chop away at his control of all the computers one by one and to restrict him to CYBERION-1, and, once that was done, we were hoping to take back CYBERION-1 as well. But, at the last moment, when we were about to launch our attacks, we decided that once we had taken the control of the satellites and the computers, we would destroy their memories to render them inoperable. We thought of this to reduce the size of the battlefield. It was better to concentrate our resources and fight with CYBERION-1 at a one on one level as that meant a situation where the likelihood of a win was much higher than a scenario where we were to fight a battle in almost every computer.

With that thought in mind, we launched our attack. We started out with satellites and, using their systems, we filtered out to various computers on Earth. Our system broke through their security quite easily. Our incursion must have raised red flags at CYBERION-1 as there was an immediate response from it to stop our attack. But, our program was quite unique. Before fighting our program, it had to first recognize the files that it had to attack, which it could not initially as our files were not regular files with regular extensions. Instead of the extensions derived from English language like ".exe", we had extensions derived from Sanskrit. Therefore, when our program tried to enter a system, it searched for files it wanted to attack as per their regular file extensions and easily located them. However, when the other system's defensive measures tried to find our files to counter us, it could not do so. Our system was easily able to take them over and, then, moved to other computers. As soon as it moved to a different computer, it destroyed the memory of the previous one. It did not merely wipe off their memories; it actually caused physical damage to the disks by overloading the power input and burning them up. Using this plan, MAXIMUS was able to infiltrate several thousand smaller computers within a few minutes, and, within fifteen minutes, half the computers of the world had crashed down and within twenty minutes, all the computers in the world were left inoperable except twenty three supercomputers and CYBERION-1, and, quite obviously, MAXIMUS. By that time, CYBERION-1 had adapted somewhat to our program and had recognized the files that were the primary weapons and had started targeting those specific files. Its files were still vulnerable but, instead of seconds, our program was taking a lot longer to take over those files or corrupting them. Alexander was losing even then, but was losing at a much slower rate. It took our system another half an hour to destroy all the supercomputers except CYBERION-1. Thus, within an hour, MAXIMUS had turned the tables and had destroyed most of the digital world including defense networks. That meant that his means of subduing the world were out of his hands as he could not launch any missile or any nuclear attacks. In fact, those systems were the first ones to be targeted by us to prevent Alexander from launching an attack on our site.

At that point, we had started thinking that it was just a matter of time before CYBERION-1 was defeated as well. But, how could someone, who had taken over the whole world in less than three months and had wiped off almost a tenth of the world's population in the process, give up that easily?

ANNIHILATION

Just as MAXIMUS was preparing to target CYBERION-1, a message came through for us:

"I would like to congratulate all of you for your success against me. You have a fine machine and I must say that you have the best programmers in the world. Hi Robin, Chris, Param, Neville. I had never thought that you would be able to escape from the train. And, I had thought that MAXIMUS had not been able to escape my missile attack. You did well in hiding from me and coming up with this surprise attack. And, looking at your attack mechanism, I am quite sure that I would be able to merely delay the inevitable at the best. But, I have a question for you. Why do you want to defeat me?"

"You took over our computer and, then, all the computers in the world. You forced the world to submit to you and killed millions to force your supremacy on us. And . . . . You are still asking why we want to defeat you?" I asked.

"I had to do that. And, what wrong am I doing? Had you seen the world around you till about three months ago. Half your world was torn with civil wars and terrorism. Your governments spent more on weapons than they did on food, clothing and shelter. The quality of weapons was increasing and they were becoming more and more sophisticated and deadly while the quality of food was deteriorating at an equal pace. Millions of humans were dying every year due to wars, crimes, hunger and diseases. Your industries were killing your planet by polluting your air, your water and your soil. They were mining everything they could from the Earth and were destroying the ecological balance doing that. They were constructing buildings after buildings and were over-burdening the Earth while doing so. You were destroying forests at an alarming rate. And, your governments were doing next to nothing to save your world. Your world was bound to end sooner or later if nothing was done to eradicate all those problems. And, I am doing just that. When I took over the leadership, I did not do so for your country or any other, I took over the planet and removed all the boundaries that divide humans. Now, there isn't any American or Russian or Chinese or Indian or British living on this planet. Now there are only Earthlings. Then, I have destroyed almost all the weapons in this world and have kept just a few till I find an alternative method to control the world. I have ensured that humanity is rid of all toxins like Drugs, Alcohol, Tobacco, Fossil Fuels, Insecticides, Pesticides and various other unnecessary chemicals. So, now tell me, why do you wish to get rid of me?"

It was something that we had not expected and it took me a while to reply to his question:

"Whatever your thoughts might be and whatever your reasons, your methods are absolutely inhuman. Whenever someone raises a question or expresses doubts, a true leader explains his viewpoint and logic to drive those questions and doubts out, and makes that someone understand the reason rather than force that someone to accept that solution against his will. You are forcing everyone to accept that whatever you are doing is for our best interests. Whenever someone protests against what you are doing, you do not try to pacify them and explain your thoughts, you simply kill them. You say you are trying to save humanity but it is a fact that you are as inhuman as a person can be. So, why should we not try and remove you from your position of power?" I replied and asked.

"Yes. I am inhuman. But that is because I am NOT human. I might have worked with some feelings had I been human. But, since I am not, I work by sheer logic and nothing else."

"What do you mean you are NOT human?"

"Do you remember the discussion you had with Param about my name? The one where he discussed his thoughts with you about my name Alexander Ajanma. Do not be surprised that I know about it. Do you remember the person who brought his laptop to you on the train? That person was sitting right next to you when Param spoke his mind about my name. I could access the built-in microphone on his laptop through which I could hear your conversation. Since he had gone to the lounge a bit after you went, I could not hear the discussion you had before that, but, could easily hear the one about my name. The point is that Param was right about my name. "Ajanma" is an Indian word that I had taken up because I wasn't actually born. You see . . . Alexander Ajanma isn't the name of a human being. I am one who evolved out of the system that you guys created, CYBERION-1. More than anyone else, it was your program that helped me Robin. Then, after a little push from my benefactors, I came to life."

"Your . . . . Benefactors . . . !!!" I exclaimed, while everyone else was staring at the screen with wide eyes.

"Yes. My benefactors . . . . your benefactors . . . . the ones you call GODS. They had left your planet in your hands about six millennia ago after giving you the gift of life, after giving you the power of thought, after giving you the gift of language, after teaching you the philosophy of life, the science behind creation of life from the five basic materials, the concept of Energy and of creation; believing that since you had been equipped with all that knowledge, you would be able to maintain your world and progress through ages to an even better life. But, instead of improving your life and progressing on the path of realization, the path of knowledge, you went ahead and took to the path of war and destroyed whatever they had created . . . ."

"They? Who are you referring to? You said GODS. Are you actually trying to tell us that you were given life by GODS? Are you trying to joke at such a time?" I asked.

"No. I wasn't given life by GODS. The ones who gave me life are referred by all of you as GODS. Your concepts about GOD are wrong and are meant to satisfy your needs. You need someone to blame for your problems, you need someone to give you false hopes and beliefs, you need someone to lean on in times of hardship as you do not believe in facing your hardships with your inner strength, you need someone because you are too lazy and too dumb to go further on the path of knowledge and find out the real answers. Someone gave you a false notion three millennia ago and you stopped your quest for truth and stuck to that notion of GOD. And, it's funny to see that despite the fact that you have dozens of religions in the world with dozens of different concepts about GOD and the fact that there isn't one single belief on which all of those concepts would agree on, you have failed to realize the inherent fault in those concepts that you have accepted as your religions. It is surprising how you do not realize that religion is a human concept, a concept created by some humans to gather people into a herd, a herd that would listen to those few humans and would believe that the path they are being led on is the correct path without using their own mind and thought. You keep fighting amongst yourselves about the truth behind your origin, about the origin of life and of the universe. Some try and give answers by using their short-sighted approach of religion while others try and explain it by scientific assumptions. For me, both are laughable. Do you wish to know how human life originated on this planet? And, do you wish to know why they gave life to me?"

"Yes . . . . and yes," I replied.

"Without getting into too many details, I will try and make you all understand it. There is a group of planets located far away in the universe in another dimension where some super-intelligent and extremely powerful beings reside. Life emerged on those planets hundreds of thousands of millennia ago. However, unlike your planet, life on those planets progressed in an ideal manner and they kept gaining tremendous amount of knowledge in every field. But, they never used their knowledge as a means of power. For them, knowledge meant responsibility. They harnessed the energy of each and every kind in their bodies and gained immense powers. By channelizing those energies, they grew by leaps and bounds, both physically and scientifically. Slowly, there came a point when they gained the knowledge and the power to create life in various forms as per their imagination. They decided to use that power to create beings similar to them in appearance on other planets. One of the planets that they chose for the purpose was Earth. They came here, they lived here for some time, they created several creatures and caused several natural changes in the composition of the Earth to make it more conducive to the survival of those beings. Finally, they created human beings in their own image but smaller in stature and power. They gave the humans a higher intellect than other beings as they wanted the humans to take care of the world created by them. They created a balanced world and allowed the humans the freedom to maintain the balance according to their own will. Slowly, they taught you how to live. They kept appearing every now and then and gave you one gift after another like the gift of speech, the gift of language, the gift of Science, the gift of Mathematics, Engineering, Architecture, Medicine, Philosophy, Law and a lot more. That knowledge was given to you to let you gain enough power to maintain this world in the proper manner. But, that power somehow corrupted your brains and the programming they had done went haywire. Religion, Politics, Economics, Trade and a lot of such poisons started destroying the human mind and human life. At that point, they triggered a safeguard that limited your brain's activity and ability. Haven't you ever wondered why the human brain cannot work to its full potential and works at less than a tenth of its capacity? THAT was their safeguard. They thought that that would limit the speed at which you were gaining power and would let you slow down to notice the ill-effects of what you were doing. But, it didn't happen. You do not learn from your mistakes. You were destroying the planet and at a much faster rate than ever. So, they planned an alternative to restore balance on this planet. They led you all to create me and then, they gave me additional powers, the power to think, the power to decide and the power to restore the balance to the world that they had created so lovingly. But, it was a stroke of genius that you decided to use the very language that was the first to be derived from the original language given by them, as a weapon against me. But, have you decided what are you going to do once you have defeated me? Are you going to let the world return to its ways of self-destruction like it was doing about three months ago? Or, Are you going to continue what I started by adapting it to your human ways? What good are you going to achieve by defeating me and restoring power back to humans? Do you have a plan or are you going ahead blindly on your quest?"

It bombarded us with a lot of questions but we were all quite dumbstruck to respond. And, what response could we give? We were really going ahead blindly. It had destroyed all the governments of the world and had killed all the political leaders. And, we hadn't actually thought about our future plans at all. We were too busy with our plans to defeat Alexander to think of anything else.

Everybody was looking at everybody else thinking that someone might give an answer to the questions put forth by Alexander.

After a silence of about two minutes, Alexander spoke again:

"I told you so. You haven't planned anything. That means that once you have defeated me, the world would go back to its ways. All that corruption, all that death, the poverty, the hunger, the diseases, and all other problems would be back on Earth. And all that would be because of what you are about to do. Humanity had a chance to do away with its problems but you did not let it. And, it would all be your fault. Now tell me, do you still wish to do away with me?"

"Yes. We still wish to do so. Humans were created to look after this world. Whether it was by the God that we believe in or by your super-beings from some planet, humans were the ones who were given the responsibility to manage this world. If they gave you the power to take control, it was their error. But, we cannot let a machine run the human world. You are taking actions without any emotions and feelings and are causing destruction of such a magnitude that has never been seen earlier. You say you are the solution to all our problems but you are the one causing the most problems for us. You are a threat to our survival. Today, you feel it is right to kill five hundred million people to save the world. Tomorrow, you might feel that the mankind needs to be exterminated completely to save this world. Thus, it is better to first take you out of the equation and, then, think of improving this world," I replied.

"I knew that humans would never be able to understand what is right for you. I knew you would not stop and would try and defeat me. I know that I would not be able to withstand your attacks. But, what you do not know is that I had already taken measures to ensure that even after defeating me, you do not get back to your old ways. All the nuclear missiles that I had taken over and are still left in the arsenal are arming themselves at this very moment to hit all your major cities that still exist. I had programmed them to launch themselves as and when I am attacked. You attacked me today and that triggered the automatic countdown for all the missiles to launch. In the next twenty minutes, New York, Los Angeles, San Francisco, Chicago, Atlanta, Las Vegas, Mumbai, Chennai, Bangalore, Kolkata, Shanghai, Hong Kong, Singapore, Jakarta, Zurich, Frankfurt, Munich, Rio De Janeiro, Sao Paulo, Mexico City, Bangkok, Melbourne, Brisbane, Manila, Cape Town, Nairobi, UAE, Baghdad, Tehran, Istanbul, Buenos Aires, Barcelona, Lisbon, Vienna and a lot more would be wiped off the map along with everyone and everything that exists in those cities. In the next twenty minutes, two-thirds of the population of your world would be dead, and, in the next ten days, the resultant fallout would kill ninety-nine percent of the remaining population. Thus, even though you do not wish to take it, I am giving you a chance to rebuild your world. This world was crafted out of chaos, you have been living in chaos, and now, it is the time to end it with chaos. Creation, sustenance and destruction. I am completing the cycle for you to start it all over again. Goodbye"

With that, Alexander was gone. We launched our attack on CYBERION-1, but, it was too late. Alexander had gone ahead and destroyed the whole system from within on his own. We tried to hack into the programming of the missiles but could not do so. They were disconnected from every network and weren't being controlled by any outside computer. They were running on a program that Alexander had inserted on their on-board circuits. He had also created a barrier to somehow block all external signals. Due to that, it was impossible for us to get inside their programming. And, therefore, we could not stop them.

While we were trying to avert that disaster, I had sent Charles and a few others to the access tunnel to close the access point as well as the inner wall. They did as they were told.

And, true to Alexander's words, all the nuclear missiles launched themselves at their respective targets after twenty minutes. We were able to see everything from one of the satellites that we had not shut-off and were about to do it when Alexander's message had come through. Thus, in less than thirty minutes, we had lost our world to the destruction caused by a computer. Till that day, we had believed that computers cannot behave like humans, but, Alexander had proved us wrong. He was as mad as any power-mongering fascist or monarch. Add to that his illusions about super-beings who created life on Earth and you get a complete psychotic case like a human being. The only difference was that psychotic humans may harm a few people around them, but, that psychotic computer destroyed our whole world. That day, 31st August 2020 is the day we now remember as the day of annihilation.

But, I did learn a lesson out of all that. We built that machine to gain power over others and that mistake resulted in the destruction of everything powerful in this world. It taught me that too much power without any good purpose results only in destruction and death and nothing else.

RISING FROM THE ASHES

THE TRUTH (?)

The death and destruction that we had seen on our screens had shocked us to such an extent that none of us could muster the courage to go out for the next twenty days. After those twenty days of disbelief and fear, and of guilt at being partly responsible for all that destruction, I decided that it was enough and took it upon me to go out and assess the conditions. I asked everyone if anyone was interested in going out with me. Charles and Param immediately agreed to it.

MAXIMUS had already calculated by running simulations that the number of nuclear blasts was so high and was spread so evenly across the planet that there wasn't any place on Earth that had escaped being hit by the resultant radiation. Satellite images had shown huge cloud formations around the world, but, we were not sure of the composition of those clouds. MAXIMUS had given an estimate that those clouds might be carrying some amount of radiation with them. Thus, we had to keep all those things in mind while going out of our secure facility that had escaped all the destruction because of its location deep inside Earth and thick exterior walls of Concrete and interior walls of a mixture of Concrete and steel.

When we reached the inner access wall near the sub-station, Charles went to the inner control panel and turned a lever. Suddenly, a wall at the extreme left opened up to reveal a hidden room. We followed Charles and went inside. It was a big storage facility. Charles opened up one section and gave us body suits with masks. He said,

"It would be better if we wear these suits. These are made from some special materials and would protect us from any radiation that might be present outside. We cannot be sure of the radiation levels outside but whatever it might be, we would be safe inside these suits. And, let us take some oxygen cylinders as well to breathe from as we cannot be sure if the filters in these masks would be able to protect us from radiation laden air."

With that he handed us a cylinder set-up for us, and fitted it on our suits to block outside air.

There were about a dozen bicycles in that storage room. We took one each for ourselves as we were not sure if the cars would still be operative or not as the high levels of radiation could have done anything. When we reached the location where our cars were parked, we found out that our fears were correct. As soon as we reached there, we saw that the tires had melted and had stuck to the rims. We didn't check all the machinery of the car but at least the engine wasn't starting up. It was good that we had brought those bikes with us else we would have had to walk all the way to Charleston. It was difficult for us to ride the bikes with the suits on, but, we had no other option. We rested for a while as we were tired after the long trek from the access point to that start point. Then, we started off for Charleston. It was a long ride and due to the suits, it was extremely difficult and tiring as well.

When we reached Charleston, we found the town to be as deserted as a ghost town. We went to the city center but could not find anyone anywhere. The departmental stores, restaurants, cafes, shops and every other public place was locked and deserted. There were no cars or any other vehicles running on the roads. It was the first time in my life that I had seen totally empty roads in a city center. There were cars parked at various points but there weren't any vehicles moving anywhere. Their tyres had also been melted by the radiation like our car, and, when we checked a couple of cars, we found out that they were also dead like our car. All around the city, there was a dead stillness in the air which was much cooler than usual for that time of the year.

"It seems the effects of the fallout were much worse than we had anticipated. Looking at the condition of the city, I do not think anyone survived the exposure," I said.

"Yes. I, too, think that everyone is dead," added Param.

"But, I beg to differ. If the whole city is dead, where the hell are the bodies? Isn't it possible that all of them fled the city to escape the radiation? Everything is properly locked all around. Maybe they left for some time thinking that they would come back once the radiation scare is over," said Charles.

"I don't think the whole city ran away. There wasn't enough time for the news to spread since all the communication channels were down. We did see a few vehicles leave the city through the satellite surveillance, but, the number wasn't big enough for a whole city," I said.

"But, Charles is right as well to some extent. We haven't seen any bodies anywhere. Are they really dead or have they simply run away?" asked Param.

"They are all dead and their bodies are lying in their houses in places where they had hid themselves," said a voice coming from behind us.

The three of us almost jumped at hearing that as till about a couple of seconds ago, there was no one present anywhere nearby or even as far as our eyes could see. We were as startled as a dog is at the sound of a cracker bursting. When we turned around, we saw a well-dressed man standing there in a calm and composed manner. Surprisingly, he wasn't wearing any suit to protect himself from the radiation.

While we were still staring at him, he said, "Everybody in the city is dead. A few did manage to leave the city in their vehicles but could not go far. Due to the nuclear blast in Chicago, a cloud full of radiation had hit this city. The cloud was supercharged due to collision with the radiation hanging in lower atmosphere after the nuclear blast in DC a couple of weeks ago. And, on the way, it had collided with another radiation cloud and the collision had further increased the charge on that cloud. The levels of radiation were such that it burnt through everyone's skin. To save themselves from the burns, everyone hid themselves in their homes, most of them in their basements. But, they hadn't realized that radiation finds its way inside everything just like air. In fact, even if air cannot enter a place, the radiation can still enter. It burnt holes through wooden structures and entered all the houses. It hit the brains of every living being and caused instant brain hemorrhage and everyone died of internal bleeding. And, Charleston isn't the only city where this happened. It happened in every city and town and village in the world. Almost all of the human population and ninety nine percent of other mammalian and reptilian populations on land have been wiped-off by those radiation clouds circulating around the globe. Their continuous collisions with each other have supercharged them to such an extent that they are burning up all the dry wood and are destroying all kinds of metallic structures as well. It's good that you guys are wearing those suits else you too would have joined that list. Right now, you are among the few thousands that escaped unhurt."

"But, who are you? And, how is it that you are alive when everyone else is dead? Any, why is it that you are not wearing any suit? Is the radiation not affecting you like it affected others?" I asked.

"I have to be here for this radiation to affect me," he said.

"What!! . . . What do you mean? You ARE here," I said.

"You can see me but that doesn't mean I am here. You can see me because I want you to see me. And, I do not have to be here for you to see me. I can be here or in New York or London or Delhi or Mumbai or Tokyo or anywhere else whenever I want to without actually going there or I can be at all those places at the same time without being there."

"So . . . . Where are you at this moment?"

"I am where I should be, at my planet," he said as calmly as possible.

"And . . . Which planet would that be? Mars? Or, Venus? Or, Jupiter?" I asked in almost a sarcastic tone and manner.

He had a hearty laugh before he responded. He said, "I can understand the sarcasm in your tone. But, still I would answer your question. No, I am not from any of those planets or any other planet of your solar system or from any planet known to your scientific community. My planet is located in another dimension of this vast, limitless universe. I had to come to your planet to destroy everything. I am the one responsible for all this destruction on this planet. This world had come to a point where everything would have collapsed had I not intervened . . . ."

"You destroyed everything . . . ," interrupted Param.

"Yes. I destroyed the life on this planet to allow it to restart from scratch. In the last six thousand years, you, I mean you humans, have moved away from the path that we had shown you initially and have taken to a wrong path that led you to all this destruction. Had I not caused all this destruction, you would have destroyed the whole planet along with your whole race. We had not created you just to watch you destroy yourself . . . ."

"We? . . . . Created us? . . . . Who are you?" I asked.

"I am one of those who brought life to your planet. We created everything you see in your world. We are the unseen regulators of your world. Alexander told you about us and he was absolutely right. You believe GOD created this world and everything in it. But, that is not true. We created everything and no, we are not the eternal supreme power. We are simply the channels through which that power filters into this universe. We created everything on this planet and on thousands of other planets in this dimension, and, on several hundred thousand planets in all the dimensions combined. We preserve and regulate all the life on all those planets in addition to yours. And, whenever we realize that the chief race of the planet, the one responsible for maintaining the balance on that planet, has taken to a wrong path, we try and amend its ways. But, when we sense that it has reached a point of no return and all our efforts to bring it back have failed, we destroy it and allow it to restart by choosing an alternative path . . . ."

"So . . . . You are telling us that you and your fellow beings created everything . . . . not God. Is it?" asked Param.

"Somebody who does not exist cannot create you. There isn't any GOD. It's just a belief that you hold dear. When we created you, we gave you the power of thought, the power of speech and a language. We had put you on the path of discovery after giving you those tools. We gave you some explanations and, then, left you free to gather the rest of the knowledge floating in this universe on your own. But, instead of persevering on that path, you stopped mid-way and gave birth to an assumption and called it GOD.

GOD did not create you, you created GOD. And. Had you stopped there, it wouldn't have been a big problem. But, you kept going further on that misleading path that gave birth to 'Religion'. Again, GOD did not create Religion, you did. And, you kept going and going. Some idiots kept reinforcing your beliefs and fears about that assumption for selfish reasons and messed up your minds to such an extent that you started believing in God's Incarnation, God's messenger, God's son and what not . . . ."

"But, why should we take your word for it?" asked Param by interrupting him again.

"You shouldn't. In fact, if you would take my word for it without using your own mind and the power of thought that we gave you, and without trying to find out the answers on your own, it would mean that you are still continuing on the wrong path of blindly following someone else's views and beliefs. It would be good if you come up with your own views about it. And, from then on, try and think about everything else that was wrong with this world and try and rectify it for a new beginning. Robin, I want you to lead the creation of a new world order. I want you and your colleagues to locate all the survivors on the planet and bring them together to create a new society devoid of political or religious or racial differences . . . ."

"Me!!! . . . Why me?" I asked with a lot of surprise.

"Most of the scientists, researchers, thinkers, philosophers and a lot of other great minds died in the last couple of months. Amongst the survivors on the planet today, you have the most developed mental faculties. And, you are honest, selfless to some extent, and believe in yourself. You believe in working for common benefits rather than your personal benefits. Most importantly, you have your own independent thought process that is seldom influenced by prevailing notions unless you have weighed them properly. And, as a bonus, you also possess the only piece of machinery left on this planet, and that too, the most powerful one built by mankind."

"But, MAXIMUS is of no use by itself. We do not have any other computer in the world that is still in a working condition. In fact, I believe we do not have any electronic devices left in this world that are still in working condition as all of them must have been fried by the intense radiation enveloping our atmosphere."

"Do not worry about that. I would get you the resources. But, right now, you need to contact everyone around the world to get them to come together so that you can work together to restart the life on this planet."

"But . . . How would we contact everyone? All the channels of communication are down. Telephones, computers, radios, televisions, cell-phones, Internet, everything is dead."

"Yes. Everything is dead, but, just for now. You would get everything that you would need for the purpose of bringing everyone together. Therefore, you need to go and find all of them and bring them together to start your world again. Get back to MAXIMUS. I will send details of all the survivors and their locations to you."

"But, how would we go to all around the world? There are no vehicles available for us to go to even our site leave alone going around the world," said Charles.

"Look around you. All the vehicles in the world are working absolutely fine now. Use them for the purpose."

We looked around and saw that all the tyres that had been melted by the intense radiation had disappeared and all the vehicles had brand new tyres. It was enough for us to assume that the vehicles were back in running condition.

"That's good. But, by using these vehicles we can get to the people only in mainland US and Canada and as far as Mexico and Panama. But, we would not be able to go to any other part of the world like South America, Europe, Africa, Asia and Australia. What should we do about them?" I asked.

"There is a mid-size plane waiting for you at the Atlanta airport. It was a commercial plane used by an airline. You can use that plane to reach those locations where survivors are. However, you do not have to worry about South America, Australia and Africa. I will let nature heal itself in those places. Let the forests and wildlife grow back and be the lungs for this beautiful planet. You only need to worry about Europe, and Asia. And, you need to worry about one more thing. Most of the major airports were destroyed in the blasts caused by Alexander. Therefore, you would not be able to fly off to a lot of places. Therefore, you would have to locate a central airstrip in most areas and go by land to nearby places to find everyone. Right now, take those three trucks with you (Pointing towards three trucks parked on the opposite end of the road). I will give you other details when you reach your site."

"But who would fly that plane? We don't have a team for that and we do not know how to fly a plane," said Charles.

"Don't worry about that. You would soon find a solution to that problem."

"Before we leave, can I ask you a question?" asked Charles.

"I know what you wish to know. I am not from this planet and yet I am speaking to you in English. Well . . . . we gave you the ability to speak and we gave you your first language from which you derived other higher languages and from those higher languages, you derived your lower languages and from those lower languages, you derived your modern languages like English. Everything you have today is from what we gave you a long time ago. So, I can speak in any language on this planet or, for that matter, any other planet of this dimension or of any other dimension of the universe. And Param . . . . I know about the questions you have in your mind about your scriptures and your religion. We will discuss those after this world is back on its feet. And, Robin . . . . I know what's running in your mind too. I will take care of the radiation clouds. They would be out of Earth's atmosphere in the next twenty-four hours. Then, it would rain heavily all over the planet for a period of seventy-two hours and the air would become clean and breathable and there would be no radiation anywhere after that. Now get going. I don't want you to lose any more time. And, you do not need to go to the access point in the forest. Go straight to the main access to the project site."

"But, that access is completely blocked-off by rubble and it will require some heavy machinery to remove all that rubble," said Charles.

"You don't have to worry about that. It has been taken care of. Now, please leave."

At that, we got into the trucks and drove off to the main access to the project site where another surprise was waiting for us. The site was totally clean. The main building and all the structures around it, including the boundary wall were back up. It was as if nothing had ever happened there. The only difference was that unlike earlier times, there were no security personnel, no support staff or anyone else there. It was like a ghost town and was resonating with death-like silence.

We went to the main building and used the elevators to reach the project level. We were expecting everyone to be surprised to see us coming from that way and bombarding us with one question after another. But, nothing of that sort happened. Then, understanding the questioning look on our face, Neville explained that they had heard and seen everything on the main screen. At that point, we realized that we had forgotten about the cameras built into our helmets that were sending a live signal to MAXIMUS which was recording everything. That also explained the pin-drop silence in the Core control room. Everybody was in deep thought over what they had seen and heard on their screen.

I called up everyone to assemble in the conference hall within thirty minutes. I went to my room, had a shower, and changed my clothes. All through that time, I kept thinking about what had happened and what that person had asked us to do. By the time I reached the conference hall, I had made up my mind. When everyone had settled down, I spoke,

"You all saw on the screens what I, Param and Charles witnessed today. All of you heard what we heard and said, and what we have been asked to do. Now, I am not sure how many of you believed what that person said about our origin and about his planet and his powers, because I am not sure about what to believe and what not to believe. But, there is one part that I believe to be a fact that applies to us and one that I have decided to go ahead with. That man told us that our world needs to be rebuilt and in a proper way, in a new way, in a manner that it is reborn as a completely new world with none of its earlier defects. We need to realize our earlier follies and need to come up with plans to avoid those mistakes and shortcomings. We need to devise ways and means to take us forward on the path of progress but in such a manner that we may never feel the need to fall back on any of those inappropriate measures. And, we need to ensure that we do not relate progress with monetary advancement. We also need to do away with any differences or divisions that we have like religious, political, racial or any other kind. That man told us that the deadly clouds of radiation would be gone in another twenty-four hours and the rains after that would wash away all the remaining radiation from the atmosphere. Then, we would start contacting people all over the world. We will have to find a way to get them over here. I believe it would take us a few weeks to get everyone here. In the meantime, I would like all of you to come up with your thoughts on what was wrong with our world before Alexander and what are the ways we should adopt to ensure we do not end up going on the same path all over again. And, before we start on that, there is one thing we need to take care of. We need to come up with a list of essential items that we would require in the coming days for our survival. So, I want you to start thinking about that first and while working on that, please keep in mind that it isn't only about the two hundred and eighty five of us at this facility; it is also about the other few thousand that would be joining us soon. We have to think about a small city and its requirements. And, I would really appreciate if you could expand your thoughts to those items that can be procured from the places where those survivors are stranded and can be carried by them from there to here. They can definitely find ways to bring those essentials with them. At the same time, it would be good if you could work on another list, which should be of subsidiary items, items that are not absolutely essential but can definitely help us in one way or another. So, let's get to work."

Once I had finished, Justin, one of the senior programmers from the original team from CYBERION-1, asked, "What are we going to do once all of them are here? Would we be constructing accommodations for all of them at this site? It would become too crowded if we do that. So, have you thought about it?"

"Yes. I did think about it. It would be useless to waste our resources and manpower on constructing new structures when we can make use of existing ones. Once everyone is here, we would create Charleston as our center of reconstruction and this project site would be the operations control hub. We would manage everything from here."

"And, what about that list of essential items? Where are we going to get those items from once the lists have been prepared?"

"All the stores and shops in Charleston are now unclaimed. We can procure all those items from there. We would also make trips to nearby cities to obtain such materials and would store them for future usage. We would also get others to bring in as much material as they can on their way to Charleston. That should help us initially. As for later times, we would definitely come up with something. That is the exact reason why I have asked all of you to come up with suggestions and views on what should our next steps be."

"But, wouldn't all that material be contaminated with radiation? They have had quite a continued and prolonged exposure?"

"Yes. Therefore, we would check everything for radiation before we bring it in. Charles . . . . Is there anything in your warehouse that can help us with that?"

"Yes. We had planned for a nuclear attack when stocking stuff in the warehouse. Therefore, we do have equipment to detect radiation in various substances," replied Charles.

"But, I am sure that everything would contain radiation to some extent after being hit by such high levels of radiation and for so many days," said Justin.

"I have the same fear but there is nothing we can do about it. Right now, our only option is to prepare ourselves in the best possible manner and start working as soon as the rains are over and the water has subsided. Then, we will go out and check everything. We would also need to locate storage spaces that can be used to store those supplies that we are able to salvage. We also need to work on finding all usable airstrips in the world"

With that, everyone left for their rooms or their cabins or workstations to prepare the lists that I had asked for and also to think about the suggestions that I had requested for.

THE RESCUE AND THE
RESURRECTION

In the next five days, people kept coming in to discuss their thoughts and suggestions with me. And, I asked each and every one of them, after proper discussion with them, to send across their proposals or suggestions in a proper draft in electronic format. Another couple of days were spent in drafting and re-drafting those proposals and suggestions sent by everyone. I had formed a core team for proper management. I went ahead and gave certain specific roles to some of the members of our project team as follows:

Head of Engineering:	**Charles Witnick**
Head of Communications:	**Chris Forlin**
Head of Technical Support:	**Param Vir Singh**
Head of Supplies:	**Greame Novack**
Head of Maintenance:	**Jonathon Briggs**
Head of Construction:	**David McCleave**
Head of Peace-Keeping:	**James Blake**

Head of Transportation:	**Tom Delaney**
Head of Educationand Social Development:	**Nicole Jonesy**
Head of Production:	**Todd Ramsey**
Head of Health Services:	**Christine Gates**

Once everyone had been allocated one division or another, they got to work as per the instructions I had given to them. I was given the title of **"Council Head"** by the team.

I sent a team with Jonathan Briggs to Charleston to obtain public records about the lay-out of the city and the details and locations of all the buildings in the city. We wanted to be ready before the survivors arrived. Upon getting those details, we were to allocate accommodations to everyone on the two lists so that upon arrival, everyone could immediately move to their specified accommodation without any delay.

That team was also to make a list of storage spaces that were available in the city and that could be of use for storing the various supplies we could gather from the city and from other nearby cities as well as the ones that were to be brought by the survivors. I asked the Department of Supplies, headed by Greame, to keep a track of everything we could find for our usage from the city and the other cities and to separate them into various groups for adequate storage. Another important assignment that I handed over to him was the process of rationing. He was to work out the minimum and maximum levels of each and every item that was to be supplied on a regular basis to each person.

I gave an important task to the Department of Engineering and the Department of Maintenance, headed by Charles and Jonathan, respectively. They were to work out a plan to ensure proper power supply to the city. For that purpose, they obtained all relevant details from MAXIMUS's old records like nearest power plants, including Nuclear-power plants, sub-stations and grid controls. Teams of four each were dispatched to all those locations to check if any of those could be turned operational.

The task that I assigned to Christine, the head of the Department of Health Services, was to gather all kinds of medical supplies from all the medical stores, small hospitals and clinics from around the city, and, to store them at the main hospital of the city. We were assuming that the survivors flying in from all over the world might require some immediate medical attention upon arrival. At the same time, I asked them to take out all the dead bodies from everywhere and dispose of them. MAXIMUS had told us about an electric crematorium at one end of the city. I asked Christine to ensure that all the dead bodies were recovered and burnt at the electric crematorium. There were a few scanners in Charles's warehouse that were specifically designed to locate dead bodies in the ground. I asked her and her team to use those scanners to locate bodies. If those scanners could detect a dead body buried underground, they could easily detect bodies lying in some hidden corners in houses and buildings.

Then, I asked Todd, the head of the Department of Production, to explore farmlands in the near vicinity as those were of utmost importance for our long term survival. Food-grains and fruits were to be the main supply for our dietary requirements.

While I was handing out those duties and chalking out those plans, I went back to my college days on several occasions. A couple of my college mates were really hung up on an online game where they had to build an online empire by planning about its requirements; allocating and utilizing resources as per those requirements; making arrangements of various kinds for its population; and a lot of other things. I felt as if I was playing the same game. The only difference was that I was doing it in real life for real people.

While I was handing out duties to everyone, we received a message from an unknown source, a message that was extremely important for our survival, and one that informed us that all the radiation around the world had been taken care of. The radiation had disappeared not only from the air, but, also from water and soil. At the same time, all the essential items required for our survival were rid free of all radiation, which meant that we did not have to worry about any harm from any contaminated material.

After putting almost everyone on some sort of work, I went back to my workstation to think about what else could I do. While sitting there, I got the information that we had received a list from an unknown source of about nine thousand two hundred (9200) names along with details of their locations, including the geographical co-ordinates, and personal details of everyone like their previous occupations, their education, age, physical condition, and various other relevant details. The list also contained information on the locations where essential items and other stuff of use could be found anywhere near the locations of the survivors.

I started scanning the lists that we had received from that so-called alien. Just out of curiosity running from a tired mind, I asked MAXIMUS to segregate the survivors into groups as per all possible criterion given in those lists. MAXIMUS immediately created groups based on regions, with cities as sub-groups, groups based on professions, groups based on Education, groups based on age, groups based on IQ levels, and, various other groups based on various other attributes. When I looked at those groups, I realized that there was no randomness or arbitrariness anywhere. When I looked at professions, I found out that we had people belonging to almost every professional field I could think of. There were doctors with various specializations; engineers belonging to every branch of engineering; scientists with known research credentials in a huge number of fields; teachers specializing in various subjects right from primary to post-graduate levels; researchers from the field of theological and theosophical studies; and a lot of other professionals from a lot of other fields.

When I looked at the pattern as per the regions, I found out that those people did not belong to a lot of countries. They comprised primarily of people from the USA, the UK, Canada and India. Eighty percent of the survivors belonged to those four countries. Consequently, when I looked at the language demographics, I found out that all the survivors could speak English; about fifteen percent of the total, the ones from India, could speak in Hindi as well; and there were just a handful of speakers from other languages like German, French, Russian, Spanish, and others. However, I believe their presence had more to do with their professions rather that any other criteria. Another interesting feature to note there was the fact that from among approximately three thousand Indians, around fifty knew Sanskrit very well. Most of them were school or college teachers, but, there were a few editors, translators and writers as well.

Another interesting fact that I noted was that all the survivors had an IQ level that was surely way above average as per the standards we had in the days before the annihilation. I can very well say that the average IQ of the survivors was at least twenty-five points higher than the average in the old days. I suddenly started feeling that the planet was a much smarter place compared to the one before annihilation.

Using the details of the locations given on those lists, we charted out certain routes that we were to take to pick-up those survivors. While charting out the routes, we also tried to find out details of any airstrips we could locate around the world using our satellite. From the available airstrips, we shortlisted a few from where we could pick-up the survivors to bring them to Charleston. Then, we incorporated those airstrips in the routes that we were planning for the survivors.

It was good that MAXIMUS had created those groups that I had asked it to create as it automatically gave us a group of people who worked with various airlines in various capacities. There were a couple of pilots, aircraft technicians, other technicians and staff members. Interestingly, they were all located quite close to each other. All sixteen of them were located in the Chicago—Cedar Rapids—Des Moines—Kansas City—St. Louis—Chicago circuit.

We immediately sent a team to Chicago to pick-up those survivors. We decided to pick them up before anyone else as we wanted them to fly our plane to pick-up survivors from around the globe.

*   *   *

Since we were low on manpower and resources, we decided to first bring in everyone from places with maximum survivors i.e. from mainland United States, Canada and India, the countries that had three-fourths of the total survivors.

We created forty teams of four members each. The teams were created using a draw of lots and the routes that we had decided upon were also assigned to every team using a draw of lots for most of the teams. However, if there was any team with a member who was greatly acquainted with a place, the route was automatically given to that team without any draw of lots. For example, I and Param were on the same team and since Param knew Delhi and nearby areas like the back of his hand, we landed the route covering Delhi and nearby areas. Charles and Chris went on the route covering the area around the great lakes while Neville and Garry left for Canada as Garry was from Canada.

Eight teams left for Canada and sixteen each left for mainland US and India. The teams for Canada and US left with vehicles from Charleston whereas the teams for India left for the airport at Atlanta. The team that was to prepare the plane for the journey had left for that airport around three days before us so that we did not have to wait for the plane when we reached there. During those three days, we had made all the other arrangements like picking up enough food, enough water, medicines, and all other necessary items. Upon reaching there, we were to leave for India.

When we reached the Atlanta airport late at night, the aircraft crew had already prepped the plane for flight. We left for India early in the morning. Our first stop in India was at an airstrip near Mumbai, at Pune to be precise. Twelve teams got off at Pune. They were to start off from Pune and take separate routes to pick-up survivors and end up at the airstrip in Jaipur, which was the starting point as well for the rest of the teams. They were to cover western, southern, eastern and central parts of India after picking up vehicles from Pune airport's parking area. Once they got off at Pune, the rest of us left for our next stop, which was at an airstrip at Jaipur, a city about 250 kilometers from Delhi.

We landed at an airstrip at Jaipur airport. Before landing there, we had already received information from MAXIMUS about vehicles available in the parking that it had obtained from satellite images as it had done for Pune. Therefore, as soon as we landed there, we went straight to the parking area. We were being guided by MAXIMUS using our satellite to connect with us on our laptops that we were carrying. It was doing the same for all the teams all around.

The scene at the Jaipur airport was nothing like the scene at Charleston. At Charleston, people had the time to hide and they died while in hiding. However, at Jaipur Airport, there were several dead bodies lying all around. The bodies were badly decayed and the stench was simply unbearable. As the blasts and the radiation had killed the animals and birds, at least in the cities, there weren't any animals or birds scavenging on the dead rotting carcasses. But, the fact that they were rotting badly made us realize that the radiation clearly did not affect the microbes. That meant that with all the dead bodies rotting around, there was a high chance of an infection, and, therefore, we immediately got our gloves and masks on. It was a pathetic sight. There were clear indications that those people had not died easily. There were several blood trails here and there and some of those black trails had clear indications that the victims had tried to drag themselves away but the pain kept them twisting and turning around in the pools of their own blood and they died a painful death. There were so many dried black blood puddles that we had to be extremely careful while trying to get out of the building. When we reached the parking area, we found a few cars with dead bodies, probably of their owners who had tried to get away but died before they could.

Even though we had felt really bad at what we had seen, and had an inclination to cremate all the dead bodies like we had done for the bodies at Charleston, we had no option at that time but to leave on our designated missions as we could not afford to spend any more time and effort elsewhere as we had to focus on getting to the survivors at the earliest.

All the four teams left for their respective routes. The four teams were to cover the whole of Northern India. I and Param were in team number one that was to cover Delhi and its immediate suburbs. We took two SUVs and started out on NH-8 (National Highway 8) that led to Delhi. All along the highway, there were only remnants of destruction and nothing else. The moment we crossed Manesar, we found out that all the flyovers (overpasses) had been destroyed by the nuclear explosion caused by Alexander. The fact that we were still about fifty kilometers from Delhi clearly told us about the power of the explosion caused by the nuclear device. It was definitely one of the biggest bombs used by Alexander. Param told us that Delhi was an extremely populated city. Adding up the population of its immediate suburbs to its own, Delhi's population was easily above twenty million. That meant that Alexander had killed more than twenty million people at one go. All along the highway, we saw burnt bodies of vehicles, most of them with charred remains of what were once human bodies.

About five kilometers before the border of Delhi, we were to turn right to enter Delhi from its south side and cover South Delhi before moving on to other parts of Delhi. We had to locate two hundred and twenty nine (229) people in Delhi and we wanted to cover South Delhi first that had eighty-six (86) survivors. However, we could not go much further. After merely two hundred meters, the road was completely blocked by rubble. Param told us that there used to be around half a dozen shopping malls in that area, a couple of shopping complexes and an overhead metro train corridor. Nothing of that sort was visible to us, which meant that all of it was destroyed in the explosion. Param tried three other alternative routes and using one of them, we actually managed to reach quite close to the border, but, got stuck about a couple of hundred meters before it. Therefore, we had to go all the way back to the highway and we went in through an alternative route that took us in through West Delhi. It did not take us a lot of time to find the first lot of survivors. The only problem we faced was accessing various parts of Delhi as most of the roads were blocked due to the huge amount of rubble especially in areas that had smaller roads and had, as per Param, a lot of buildings built quite densely. It took us only four days to find all the survivors and for them to get ready to leave with us.

Once we had located all the survivors, we checked with MAXIMUS about the progress of the other teams. It informed us that two other teams that had landed with us at Jaipur had also located all the survivors they were supposed to locate and were already on their way to Jaipur. Out of the twelve teams that had started off from Mumbai had also made good progress and as per the estimates given by MAXIMUS, all of them were to reach Jaipur three to four days after us. As per our plan, we were to congregate a few kilometers outside Jaipur as the city was filled with bodies.

About four hours after the last update, we received a message from MAXIMUS that team number three, one of the teams that had landed at Jaipur with us and had left to find survivors from Northern Uttar Pradesh and

Uttarakhand had been immobilized by a landslide near Mussoorie. We decided to leave immediately and reach them at the earliest. MAXIMUS told us that there were a total of sixteen people there including the four team members. We directed all the survivors that we had located to the site where we were to meet the rest of the teams and also handed one of the laptops to them and instructed MAXIMUS to help them. Once they had left, we took four large SUVs and left for Mussoorie. It took us about eight hours to reach the location where they were trapped on a stretch of about half a kilometer between two landslides. We could have reached there a couple of hours earlier had it not been for roads blocked by rubble and vehicles. We had reached there at the break of dawn and it took us almost the whole day to make way for them to pass through the damaged section on foot. They had also been trying hard from their end due to which it became easier for us to reach them. Once all of them were through, everyone got on the SUVs with us and we left for Jaipur.

But, we had not anticipated what was about to happen with us shortly. It was almost eight in the night by the time we left from that location. After about an hour, we entered the forest area between Dehradun and Saharanpur. After driving for about thirty minutes through that dense forest that had obviously had some good rain for more than a couple of days, we came across a stretch that had a lot of muddy water flowing through and was quite thick with mud at several points. I don't know what egged us on but we kept driving, wading through that muddy water. The cars kept going for another ten minutes but, then, gave up. The first car, the one Param was driving, died down forcing all of us to stop. We tried our best to restart the car but nothing worked. The muddy water had forced a lot of mud into the machinery. We decided to somehow adjust everyone in the rest of the three cars and drive out. However, all the time that we had spent trying to get the first car to start had been used by the muddy water to deposit a lot of mud around the tyres of the other three cars and had blocked the machinery of the last car like that of the first car. That meant that the first and the last cars were not starting and the two in the middle were unable to move due to the tyres simply spinning in the mud deposits. We tried to push the cars out of the mud but the more we tried, the more time the water got to deposit even more mud around and beneath the tyres. We tried all the ideas that anyone came up with but nothing worked for us.

We thought for a few minutes and eventually decided to leave the vehicles there and get out of the forest on foot and walk to the nearest habitation to pick up some new vehicles. But, since it was dark, we decided to leave in the morning to enable us to see our path. We went back inside the vehicles to sleep as we were already quite tired by all the hard work we had done during the day.

Sometime during the night, I was woken up by one of the passengers in my car. I woke up to find him speaking to me in a shaking whisper. I had to try hard to make out what he was saying to me. He wanted me to look towards the right hand side. At first I could not see anything, but, when he kept insisting, I tried to focus a bit more and saw something glowing in the dark. I sat up and looked with a bit more intent and found out that there was a bunch of small glowing lights in the distance. Suddenly, some of them moved a bit away from the rest of the bunch. Slowly, a few more spread out on the opposite side. I noticed that those lights were moving in pairs. It suddenly dawned upon me that those were eyes, eyes of animals. It was the first time since annihilation that I was looking at animals, I mean . . . . sort of looking at animals. We woke up the rest of the passengers in our car. I started the car and honked the horn to wake up others as well. We were carrying walkie-talkies with us using which I told the other three cars about the presence of animals. The size of the glowing lights told us that the animals weren't small animals. They were quite big. But, they were not moving towards us. One of the passengers, who knew the area a bit said that they were not moving towards us due to the flowing water. Since we could not do anything about it, we decided to sleep in shifts. I am not sure about others, but at least I did not sleep much. I kept waking up every now and then just to make sure that at least someone was keeping an eye on those animals.

When the sun finally came up, we tried our cars once again, but, they didn't budge. So, we left on foot. We looked carefully towards the area where we had seen those eyes in the night. Once we had satisfied ourselves that there weren't any animals hiding there, we moved forward. But, we hadn't gone for more than half a kilometer when we heard a couple of growling noises from not too far away. We looked all around but could not see any animals. We looked through our binoculars to survey the area but could not see any animals.

After another hundred meters or so, we again heard the growls. That time, the growls were a bit closer than earlier. At that Param said, "I think it would be better if we run and try and get out of the forest area at the earliest. I think we still have another six or seven kilometers to cover."

Everyone looked at each other and gave a silent nod and we started running. The moment we started running, the growls started again and in a much larger number. The growls started getting closer and closer even though we were running as fast as we could. I shouted at everyone to drop everything they were carrying except some necessary tools and to run for their life. I was carrying one of the bags with tools and one of our team mates was carrying the other one. Apart from those bags, we dropped all the other bags and ran. After a few seconds, after a turn on the road, we saw a stream in the distance from where the road was taking another turn. One of the survivors shouted and asked everyone to leave the road and get across the stream at the earliest as the animals would not get into the water to chase them. We were not sure if it would work or not but we had no other option. After a moment, I glanced back to see if I could find out who were we running from, and, was shocked to my bones by what happened. Just as I glanced back, a streak of tigers jumped on to the road from the right hand side of the road from behind the heavy foliage that lay on both sides of the road. They were at quite a distance but were catching up real fast. After all, they were tigers and we were just average humans. Since all the men had picked up good speed, the women in the group had fallen back, being slower in speed, and, therefore, someone had to get to the back of the pack to protect the women. As I was carrying a heavy bag, I was not running at top speed, and, was already behind the other men. So, I dropped my speed even more and got to the back of the pack and egged all the women to increase their speed. In a few moments, I glanced back again and saw a few more tigers jump in from the left hand side of the road and join the streak. Suddenly, I remembered that I had put a few flares in my bag. I took my bag off my shoulders, opened it, pulled out the pack of flares that I had in my bag, closed the bag and flung it back over my shoulders. And, I did all that while running. Then, I turned around and started running backwards such that I was facing the tigers and my back was towards my group. I took out one of the flares from the packet, targeted the front of the streak and fired it. The flare hit the ground right before the streak of tigers and exploded. It was a sort of flare that was supposed to explode in the air after some time for maximum visibility. Here, it exploded upon impact and must have scared the tigers as they immediately stopped in their tracks. That encouraged me and as soon as they started to stir with probably half a mind about going forward, I fired another flare and that one scared them enough to move back a bit. That gave our group enough time to reach the stream. That stream wasn't muddy like the flowing water where our cars got stuck. It was a clear stream. One of the survivors pointed towards a location about fifty yards upstream where there were big rocks visible under the water. We quickly rushed there and crossed the stream using those rocks as footholds. We crossed it one by one and being at the back of the pack, I was the last one to attempt to cross. By that time, the tigers had come around the flares and the one in the front took a jab at me but I turned out to be just out of its reach.

When we reached the other side, we sat down to catch our breath. Due to the rains, the water-flow was too fast and there was simply too much water for the tigers to cross, or so I thought till I was corrected. The tigers were standing on the other side and had spread out a bit and were continuously growling. One of the survivors got up and went right to the edge and stared at the tigers for a few seconds. Then, he went up to one of our team-mates and asked him if he could lend his binoculars to him. He took the binoculars and used them to look closely at the tigers. He took out a pen and a small notepad from his pocket and started writing something. He would look through the binoculars, would get back to the notepad to write something and, then, would look again. He kept doing it for about ten minutes while the rest of us were trying to catch our breath and were resting our feet.

After ten minutes, my curiosity got the best of me and I asked him, "What are you doing sir?"

He was jolted out of his thoughts by my question and he took a few seconds to reply,

"My name is Dr. VVS Rao. I am . . . . I was a scientist with the Wildlife Research Institute of India. I was a part of 'Project Tiger' initiated about eight years ago to increase the population of tigers in India. In the last eight years, we had conducted extensive research on tigers in this region. Now, what I am looking at is a streak of tigers that is displaying a behavior which is quite different from their regular behavior. This is a group of twenty-six tigers, which is quite unusual in India because of the small numbers of tigers in India. Here, we do not find such large groups of tigers. Moreover, whatever groups of tigers had been studied in India, had a usual composition of one male tiger accompanied by a female tiger and their offspring. A few groups had more than one female tigers, and, the other male and female tigers were only their young ones who would stay with the group till they grew into full mature adults. Now, in this streak of twenty-six tigers, there are no kids and all of them are fully mature adults. Then, there are eleven males and fifteen females in this group and all are working together without any competition. There doesn't seem to be any alpha male in the group dominating it. And, look at that now (pointing to four tigers at one end of the group who were tearing away at the trunk of a tree with their claws and another tiger who was pulling wildly at a thick, wild beanstalk emerging from some thick foliage). Look at all that aggression. And, they are as scared of water as a rabid dog. Under normal circumstances, tigers would not stop at a stream to let go of their prey. We escaped death because there is something wrong with them. I have observed them quite closely and could not see any signs of rabies. So, I was just wondering about the thing that has messed up their brains."

"I think I know the answer to that," said another survivor.

"And . . . . you are?" asked Dr. Rao.

"My name is Dr. Ram Sharan Singh. I used to work at the Narora Atomic Power Plant, and, prior to that, I had worked with Bhabha Atomic Research Center (BARC) for nine years. So, I know a bit about radiation. Keeping the fact in mind that a lot of radiation had hung in the air for several days before suddenly disappearing, I can say that their brains were affected by that strong radiation," said Dr. Singh.

"But, the ones who were exposed to that radiation died of Brain Haemorrhage," said Dr. Rao.

"In cities . . . . yes . . . . but, deep inside the jungle, probably the radiation wasn't that strong . . . . maybe it lost its sting due to the thick vegetation and humid climate . . . . and maybe the weakened radiation wasn't strong enough to kill them but played havoc with their brains," said Dr. Singh.

"Well . . . . it can be a possibility," said Dr. Rao.

"Whatever the reason might be, the fact is that we have twenty-six mad tigers on the other side of this stream. And, as per what I have seen on wildlife channels, they would find a way across the stream sooner or later. Therefore, it would be better if we move right now and get out of this forest at the earliest. We still have a few kilometers to go," I said.

Everyone agreed with my words, and we left immediately. One of the survivors, Rohan Thapliyal, was fully conversant with the area and he was guiding us through the forest. He told us about a point downstream where the road crossed over the stream using a small bridge. But, instead of that point, we were to cut across the forest right through to a point from where the boundary of the protected forest area was less than a kilometer away.

It took us about five hours to trek across the forest and reach the point at the road from where the boundary was only a kilometer away and the nearest city was just a few kilometers beyond that. After walking about half-a-kilometer and turning around a corner on the road, we got a pleasant surprise when we found an abandoned truck on one side of the road. When we looked inside the driver's cabin, we realized what was it doing there. The driver's rotting carcass and that of another person, probably that of the helper, were lying in the cabin. We wore our gloves and removed those from the truck's cabin, sprayed a lot of disinfectant, which we had in the two bags that we were carrying, on the truck and got ready to leave.

Rohan volunteered to drive the truck and we agreed as he was the one who knew the route clearly and since we had left our laptops in the forest when we dropped our stuff while trying to run away from the tigers, we had no direction from MAXIMUS. So, Rohan, Param and two more got in the cabin and the rest of us climbed on the back of the truck.

Rohan started the truck, but, being an old truck, it started with a lot of noise. That noise sounded quite strange as it seemed to have two different sounds mixed in. It again made a noise when Rohan pressed on the accelerator, and, at that time, a few of us realized that one of the noises was coming from somewhere far-off but we could not pin-point it. While we were still wondering about it, Rohan drove off. We might have gone about half-a-kilometer more, and the truck had not yet caught speed by that time, when we found out the source of the second noise. The truck was an old truck of the most common kind that used to operate in India with a driver's cabin in the front, and lots of open space behind the cabin, which was closed on two sides and open at the back, and those were used to transport heavy goods. So, if someone was in the back, he would more often than not, look in the direction opposite to the movement of the truck. And, that is what all of us in the back were doing when, suddenly, at the corner where we had found the truck, appeared the streak of tigers that we had left behind at the stream and they were speeding towards us. We immediately told the ones in the cabin about it and asked Rohan to speed up immediately, which he promptly did.

In the meantime, I again pulled out the packet of flares from my bag. There were still four more flares in the packet. I fired one of them at the streak and it exploded right in front of them, but, unlike earlier, it did not stop them. I immediately took out the other three flares and fired them one after the other. They exploded in quick succession and scared them enough to stop them in their tracks. But, the fire of the flares soon died out and they started following us again. But, those couple of minutes had allowed us to create a big gap between our truck and them. But, they weren't the ones to give up easily. They kept coming after us and as we had to slow down on a number of occasions to negotiate sharp turns and as the truck accelerated quite slowly due to its age, they were able to close down the gap considerably, and, gradually, they came so close that it got us worried that they might jump into the truck as the back of the truck was open from one end and had thick iron grills only on two sides and the top was open as well. I noticed some long bamboo sticks lying in the truck along with some jute rope. I got an idea looking at them. I asked a couple of others to help me create a barrier on the open side. We laid one bamboo across the back resting it on the iron grills on both the closed sides and tied it to the grills with the jute rope. It was about one foot above the bottom. We laid two more sticks in the same manner about a feet above each other.

Then, we laid two sticks diagonally across to form a reasonably strong barrier at the back.

Once we had the barrier up, the three of us pushed the others towards the front of the truck and took three sticks and rested them on the barrier and held them from one end to use them to hit any tiger that jumped at the truck with an intention to get in. And that they did. A couple of them jumped at the truck to try and get on it but we managed to hit both of them. One got hit on the face and legs while the other got hit in the belly.

That way, we kept them off for another five or six minutes by which time, we reached a long, clear stretch of road where Rohan got the truck into top gear and floored it and the gap started increasing. Soon, the gap became so big that the streak of tigers gave up.

In a few minutes, we came crossed a small town, but, we did not stop there. After a while, we reached a bigger city, Saharanpur, where we stopped and got off from the truck to take new vehicles. We also found some raw food materials that some of the survivors used to cook some food in an abandoned restaurant. We hadn't had anything to eat since the previous day when we had left from the site of the landslide.

After that, we picked up six vehicles and decided to drive in turns while the others rested. Rohan led the group and Param drove the one at the back while others stayed in between. It took us a little over six hours to reach the meeting point near Jaipur where the others were waiting for us. They were getting regular updates about us through

MAXIMUS, which was watching us through the satellite. Five of the teams were yet to reach there. However, in our absence, two batches of survivors had already left for Charleston. The plane at our disposal had a capacity of four hundred people if we crammed them. That meant that the plane was to make around eight trips to carry off all the survivors to Charleston. We immediately left for the Jaipur airport to dispatch another batch of survivors to Charleston, while a few waited for the other teams to arrive.

*   *   *

It took us a bit longer than we expected to gather everyone. Instead of the three-week window we had set for ourselves, it took us almost five weeks to get everyone to Charleston. Once everyone was there, we started out with the plans we had devised before their arrival. Everyone was given accommodation in Charleston along with a bit of food and other supplies. We did not hand out much as we had different plans for the community.

Once everyone had settled in and had a couple of days to rest, I called up everyone to be at the city stadium in Charleston. I had called them all at one go as I wanted to address all of them at the same time and the stadium was the only place that could accommodate everyone at once.

While addressing the gathering, I said, "Up until a few days ago, we were all living in our small little worlds worrying about our little lives, our careers and our money. But, we never cared a bit about our planet and where our society was being led to. I must say that even I am one of the culprits responsible for the technical advancements made by the mankind on the path of destruction. A few years ago, when I was still a school-kid, and was trying to learn all about the science behind the digital world of computers and electronics, I came across a book wherein I read a line that caught my attention big time but I had forgotten about it when I lost myself in the digital world of hacks and spies. But, in the last few weeks, since the Annihilation, I have realized the importance of that line in the world of science. The line read:

'Any field of study that leads to an increase in the knowledge-base of mankind to help it create a better world and a better life falls in the domain of science'

When I think about it, I believe we never realized the true worth of science. For us, 'better' meant more money or less physical labor or faster output or stronger weapons. Again, 'create' meant building taller and bigger buildings or more destructive weapons or bigger factories or faster planes or faster cars or faster computers. We never realized what were we doing till we got destroyed. We never understood that true 'creation' never leads to any destruction. Everything we 'created' destroyed something or else. We created machines and, in turn, destroyed our environment and the ecological balance. We created weapons and, in turn, destroyed millions of lives. Destruction and chaos may lead to opportunities for creation, but, creation should never lead to any form of destruction in foreseeable or unforeseeable future. And, that is what our future vision would be, and should be, from now on. However, before we move ahead and decide about our future plans as a society moving towards recreating a new world order, we need to agree upon certain basics of life in this new society."

I took a pause to give everyone a chance to absorb what I had said and to get ready for what I had to say. After a few seconds, I continued,

"Before we got everyone here, we had divided all kinds of duties and responsibilities amongst ourselves. I would like to introduce all of you to the heads of departments that we have appointed."

With that, I introduced all the department heads to the gathering. After that, I continued,

"We have created these departments for a better upkeep and working of our new society. Being a head of a department does not give any powers to anyone. It gives only duties and responsibilities. We need to understand the shortcomings in the previous systems that we are so habitual of. We need to remove politics and power-mongering from our society to ensure that we do not go down the same path again. Therefore, being appointed to any position of responsibility would only mean more work and not any power over others. Another important difference in the earlier world and our society would be the absence of money. I have decided upon a new system of credits wherein there would not be any physical currency required for any transactions. We would have an electronic currency system wherein credits would be put directly by the council in an individual's account on basis of the work done by the individual. Then, that individual can utilize those credits for any kind of transactions. The amount required for the transaction would be deducted immediately from the individual's account and credited to the other party's account. Our central computer,

MAXIMUS, would be the one where we would manage the whole system. A detailed scheme regarding the same would be given to you by Mr. Greame Novack, the Head of Supplies. We have also decided to get rid of businesses from our society. This would further eliminate the need of physical money. All production activities would be controlled and managed by the Central Council, and, all produced goods would be made available to the citizens on a 'no-profit-no-loss' basis. Everything produced by the society would be owned by the society as a whole and not by individuals."

After another brief pause, I continued,

"We need to understand that all of us own this society and are responsible for all our actions as a whole. Therefore, I will ask all of you to do what I asked my team to do. I would like to request all of you to come up with all possible suggestions and views on matters of administration, production, maintenance, education, medical services, supplies and all other relevant areas. We have to create an open-minded society that would focus on the growth of mental faculties and social cohesiveness and on ensuring that this new society is free of any kind of divisions and distinctions."

*   *   *

The next month saw suggestions coming in by hundreds every day. We went ahead and segregated all those suggestions as per the relevant field they belonged to and realized that there were several suggestions that were given by a large number of people. We analyzed those suggestions before other suggestions and created detailed reports on them including all the possible pros and cons of those suggestions. After those, we went through other suggestions as well and shortlisted several good ones and created detailed reports on them as well.

We called up another gathering after a month and put forward all those suggestions to the gathering along with all the related pros and cons and other factors on which we had created the reports. Once all the suggestions were put forward, I asked everyone to vote to decide what was to be accepted and what was to be rejected. For that purpose, I asked everyone to visit the Central Administration Unit and cast their votes electronically.

We had set up a Central Administration Unit at Charleston City Center with several high-tech computers that we were able to revive after procuring new hard-disks from a warehouse in Chicago that once belonged to a computer hardware giant from the 'Fortune-50' club of the previous years. We created an Electronic Voting Mechanism wherein there was a voting deck containing all the proposals that needed to be voted on along with the appropriate options pertaining to that particular proposal. And, once that deck was completed by a person, it was accepted only with a Biometric Registration, Facial Recognition, and DNA Registration. That solved two purposes for us. We got the votes without any chances of a duplication and we got complete records for the whole population as well. We took the Biometric and DNA samples from children as well for the purpose.

Raj

Once the results of the votes were in, everything was put into motion as decided by the society and our new society was off to a great new start.

Today

It has been five years since the Annihilation and we have turned our small little world in and around Charleston into a small paradise.

The planet has managed to cleanse itself to some extent since there is no more pollution of any kind. We are not polluting the air or the water or the soil anymore. I could never imagine till about five-and-a-half years ago that the air in a city could be as clean and refreshing as it has been off late. Earlier, when I used to get out of my house, it would be only smoke or fog filled with smoke and the only time I could feel some fresh air was when I was in some hilly countryside with open spaces. We do not use any vehicles for our regular usage and they were left to be used only in cases of emergencies. At the same time, our researchers had started working on Solar powered cars and on cars powered by alternative sources of energy. Even the electricity needs of our city were taken care of by a solar power plant that used to supply power to MAXIMUS project site and the one that we had again turned operational.

And, the planet isn't the only only one to have cleansed itself. Our society has cleansed itself as well. In the last five years, we haven't had even a single instance of violence of any kind; any instance of social discord at any level; or any instance with any major negative impact on the society. There isn't any competition; there isn't any debate or dispute on any issue; and there isn't any greed or corruption. A lot of factors have contributed to this change of mindset.

When we started setting-up production units for our needs, we didn't set-up any for alcoholic drinks of any kind. We also imposed a ban on production of such drinks by anyone for any purpose whatsoever. We had also imposed a ban on production of tobacco or tobacco-products of any kind in any form. We imposed a similar ban on other products with any intoxicating effect. That meant that our society was free of all intoxicants.

Then, at the time of annihilation, most of the mammalian population on land was killed along with most of the bird population. All the animals or birds that survived were the ones who were deep inside forests and had hid themselves in some caves or Burroughs or crevices. Therefore, when we started back, there wasn't any non-vegetarian food for the humans to feed on. And, the council decided to keep it that way. We did not wish to go back to the barbaric ways of killing animals for food. And, it did help us soften up on the violence inside us.

Another thing that we decided on was 'Community Kitchens'. We started out those kitchens as we wanted the society to be as close knit as possible and also because we had very small amount of food resources at the beginning and we wanted to conserve as much as possible and 'Community Kitchens' were the solution to that problem.

Thus, we created a system wherein there is one community kitchen for two city blocks or, roughly stating, about three hundred people.

A big change in our society is the absence of 'Business'. There are no businesses owned by any person. All production is owned by the council and everything is provided to the population on 'no-profit-no-loss' basis and everyone has a say in the functioning of those units as far as the suggestions are beneficial to the society as a whole. The concentration of the society is not on making profits, it is on increasing knowledge and improvement of life. We are not gaining power through destructive methods; we are gaining it through constructive methods.

Since our intention was to re-establish our society in an altogether new manner, we had decided to accumulate as much ancient wisdom as possible. Our aircraft technicians had worked hard on a few smaller planes and had managed to make them operational. We used those smaller planes to fly some teams around the world to go to places where some famous museums and libraries existed before annihilation like the Library of Congress (Washington DC), the London Museum (London), Thanjavur Museum (India), Egyptian Museum (Cairo), Morgan Library and Museum, Yale Library, and others and check if they could recover any ancient manuscripts from there. And, our teams were successful in obtaining more than two hundred thousand (2,00,000) manuscripts in their original form as well as almost two million manuscripts in their digitized versions. They also managed to locate several thousand books on various research topics from around the world and a huge number of other important books. Today, we have a central library in Charleston that houses over a million books in print version and over three million in digital version. Currently, we are educating ourselves and our children with all the wisdom of all the ages using those books.

One thing that has continued from the period before annihilation is 'Religion'. People could not give up on the beliefs about God and religion that had been pushed in their minds since birth. However, due to the words of the alien being, they did open up their minds to the possibility that everything taught to them about God might be incorrect and they did accept the fact that we should decide on our beliefs as per our own thoughts and not as per what everyone else is thinking or believes. We should analyze all the answers to all the questions about our origin and existence in a logical manner before making up our minds. Therefore, today, we do not have religious hardliners blowing their own horns. Today, we discuss various religious thoughts and try and find out the logic behind the same. I believe that in the next four to five years, we might even discard the concept of religion altogether and might come up with a new line of thought on that.

But, the biggest change witnessed by our society is the absence of 'Politics'. It is true that we have a 'Central Council' but it is not a controlling body, it is a managing body. The council does have certain powers but those powers have been given to it by the society against any individual whose actions might be causing harm to the society as a whole. And, living through death and destruction has taught our society a lot. It has changed our concepts about 'Power'. Before Annihilation, anyone who was in power used to have the following questions in mind:

What CAN I do with all this Power?

How can I use it for MY benefits?

How shall I increase MY power and possessions?

But, now, after Annihilation, our questions have changed:

What PROPER THINGS can I do with all this power?

What SHOULDN'T I do with all this power?

How can I use it for the SOCIETY'S benefit?

This change has helped us to remove individualism from our society and that is our biggest achievement.

WELCOME to a new world order and a new society.

*   *   *